Bad Decisions

By: Alexander Martin

Author Note:

This is a work of fiction, none of the characters are real or are they based on real people or events. Please do not take the actions or expressions noted in this story as the Author's outlook on life or respected behavior of anybody alive or deceased.

Please have fun and enjoy reading these stories.

Chapter One: Living in The Past

I looked into his eyes as he pushed deeper into me. My legs were high on his shoulders as he looked down at me and fucked me hard. I love watching his steel blue eyes as he fucked me.

"Harder," I said as his thick cock slammed into me repeatedly.

I felt his balls slapping against me as he fucked me as if his life depended on it.

"Harder, Jacob!" I said as I looked up at him.

"You have to get up," Jacob said as he smiled at me.

"What?" I asked.

"Your alarm is going off," Jacob said to me.

I sprung up as my dream faded, and the reality of the divorce sunk in. I looked over at the alarm and turned it off.

Jacob and I had been divorced for over two years, but I still had the recurring dream of our last time in this bed.

"Fuck," I said as I sprang out of bed and started to get ready for the day.

I looked in the mirror before I went into the shower. My dark black hair was all over the place. Jacob loved to pull on my hair. He loved how dark it looked. Even now, at thirty-six, it was still holding its color; sure, there was a bit of gray here and there, but nothing was getting out of hand.

He also loved my huge boobs. I had always been blessed or cursed, as some would put it, with huge tits. As soon as puberty hit, it was like mother nature said, *'Here you go bitch!'* and dropped me from the boob tree and made sure I hit every branch on the way down.

By the time I was a sophomore in high school, I was much bigger than all the other girls and most of the teachers. Ms. Tuean was the only woman in the school bigger than me, but in my defense, she was big all around. Add to that a nice ass, and I was the envy of most girls in high school.

Jacob and I started flirting with each other after we graduated high school. Nothing came about it for a few years as we were total opposites. He was a geek, and I was into jocks. But the flirting was fun, and one day at a red-neck party out in the woods past our town, it led to other things.

Who knew a geek like him had a huge white cock. It was the thickest and longest I had ever seen, and that said a lot for me.

I was no prude in high school and didn't hold anything back after I graduated. I took Jacob's virginity right there in the middle of nowhere out in the woods.

What happened next was unexpected. Even though we used protection, I became pregnant. Many of the guys hoped it was theirs as they would have the freak in the sheets all men wanted, but I knew it was Jacob's.

Jacob proposed the moment I told him I was pregnant. He didn't even ask if it was his or not, he knew the lifestyle I had led, and even with that, he still wanted to marry me. That was just over eleven years ago, as our son Clayton had just turned eleven two months ago.

I quickly got ready and headed to work. I worked at a small warehouse down by the railroad tracks. I did payroll, as well as many other things.

The only good thing about the divorce was that we co-parented well. Besides, Jacob wanted nothing to do with me unless it concerned Clayton.

I couldn't blame him; the divorce was my fault. No, if's or buts about it.

Jacob used to work as a tech for a local warehouse, but then he found a much better job working for a larger tech company. The problem was that he always left to go out of town weekly.

At first, I looked past it due to the amount of money Jacob made, which provided us with a lovely house and even better vehicles.

Jacob knew how high my sex drive was and had no problems when he would come home to find that I had bought new toys to keep me going while he was gone.

Along with my job at the warehouse facility, I worked part-time at a bar. Something to keep my mind occupied, plus I liked to flirt with some of the guys. Nothing would ever come of it, but it was nice to tease.

One night after closing, things went too far. I should have gone straight home and not hung out with friends.

Like in high school and afterward, I hung out with the wrong crowd, and that night we went bar hopping in the city.

We didn't live in a small town, far from it, but it does have a tight-knit community where everybody knows everybody. So going to the central city is a forty-minute drive on the highway, which for us was nothing as most of the bars closed at eleven in our part of town.

Well, I got toasted, completely and utterly wasted. Jacob was out of town, and Clayton was having a sleepover with friends, so I took the opportunity to be as wild as possible, which for me, was absurd.

I did many things wrong that night. One of them was that I stood up in the back of my friend's pick-up truck and flashed everyone as we drove down the strip of bars.

It wasn't until we got back that things went from bad to worse. I had always had a thing for guys with tight rock-hard abs, and Johnny, a friend of a friend, was with us. He worked out a lot, so when we were at Kate's house by the pool, he took off his shirt. I was totally out of order.

It started with all of us jumping into the pool topless. Which wouldn't have been wrong, I had been known to flash my giant tits at the drop of a dime, but when Johnny came over to me at the side of the pool staring at my tits, it was over.

Not even ten minutes later, I was sucking Johnny's cock as he sat at the pool's edge. I was still in the water between his legs, sucking his cock like it was the last one on earth with everyone watching.

My friend Kate tried to stop me, but I was too far gone to care. I sucked his cock until he came into my mouth.

Johnny held my head down with both hands, shouted, and cheered as his friends yelled Johnny! Repeatedly. He held my head down hard until he was totally spent.

Then, when everyone started laughing and calling me a cheater and a whore. Some of them even wanted me to suck them. It was only then I realized what I had done. I rushed out of Kate's house and drove home.

When I got home, I could still taste the cum on my tongue and smell it on my breath. I tried to wash it all out. I kept wishing it hadn't happened, that it was some fucked up mistake that I could erase, but it did, and as soon as Jacob returned, everyone would tell him.

None of the people there at the time were loyal to me, nor were they good friends, except for Kate, who had tried to stop me.

I called Kate right after I took a shower, she came over, and I cried in her arms as she tried to calm me down. There was no way this was going to end well.

Jacob returned home, and he was already fuming before he even got in the door. I wanted to tell him first, but it's not something you can say over the phone. I knew I had to tell him, but someone got to him first, and the moment he walked in the door, our marriage was over.

I got it all from Jacob's parents, who were still alive and well and still married.

My parents were both deceased. They lived terrible lives and died in a tragic car accident while under the influence.

They always said the apple doesn't fall far from the tree, and here I was, making the same mistakes they did, making bad decisions while drunk.

"Did you get my report?" my boss Charles asked as he entered my office. Instantly bringing me back to the present.

I blindly lifted a piece of paper and handed it to him. My job was easy. Most of the time, I sat at my desk, typed out reports, and sent emails.

Charles was one of the few that still talked to me. Most people who knew me blamed me or called me names under their breath. I deserved it; I made no problems for Jacob when he filed. I signed the papers and gave him what he wanted, space. He wanted nothing to do with me, so I gave him all the space he needed.

I didn't expect that space would put him right in the arms of my friend Alyssa. She swooped in and took him before the ink was completely dry on the papers.

Now the two of them lived just down the road from me, and if the rumors were true, they were planning on getting married.

Jacob loved Alyssa because she was the perfect woman. She never went out drinking. She went straight home after work and didn't hang around with any guys unless she was with Jacob. She was perfect for him.

I picked up the phone and called Jacob. I wanted to know when to pick up Clayton, as it was my weekend to have him.

"Hey," Jacob said as he answered.

"What time should I come around?" I asked.

"Seven?" Jacob replied.

"Sounds good," I nodded.

"Any plans?" Jacob asked.

"Well, I work tonight and tomorrow at the bar," I said as I leaned back in my chair. "But Sunday, I was thinking of taking him to the archery range. He has to get used to his new bow."

"He will like that," Jacob replied.

This was our usual conversation. It was always centered around Clayton, never about us, not about me, not about him or his relationship. Everything was about our son.

"Oh, do you know any good guys that could come out and look at the deck?" I asked.

"Shit!" Jacob said. "My fault I completely forgot about that, sorry."

"Not a problem, it's still shaking, and Clayton forgot about it and went outside, and he said it felt like it was going to fall apart," I said.

"Yeah, it would be best to stay off it," Jacob replied. "Tell you what," he paused.

Which only meant he was going to say something I wouldn't like. He always paused when he was going to say something about Alyssa.

"Say it," I nodded.

"Jesse knows a few good workers that are really cheap," Jacob said. "He was the one we went to when we added that extra room to the house."

Jesse was Alyssa's brother and one of the guys at the pool that night. I was sure he was the one that told Jacob before I could. He never admitted it, but I knew it had to be him.

"Sure," I nodded as if he could see me. "It has to get done," I admitted more to myself than to him.

"Cool, I will tell him to swing by this weekend?" Jacob asked.

"Definitely," I said. "I better get back to work, before Charles throws a tantrum," I said.

Charles was putty in my hands. I often got away with whatever I wanted as long as the paperwork was all done, and the payroll was done by Thursday.

I fumed for over an hour, even though I had no one else to blame for the downfall. It still made me mad that I wasn't the one to tell him.

I still had feelings for Jacob. Kate always said it was because of the sex, but it was much more than that. I missed him as a person.

It had been two years, and I hadn't dated or even thought about another person except for Jacob. And now he would be out of reach for good if he married that bitch.

Alyssa was the opposite of me. She was skinny and fragile. She loved running marathons. Taking Jacob and Clayton all over the place to see her run. She also competed in that iron man contest. She used to be the friend that tried to keep everyone in line. Where was she when I needed her?

If Alyssa had been at the party, she would have yanked my head off Johnny's dick and pulled me out to my car by my hair. I loved Kate, but yelling for me to stop wasn't going to stop me.

"HEY BUDDY," I SAID as I picked up Clayton.

"Hey," he said as he climbed into the passenger seat.

I waved at Jacob as he went back into their house.

"So, what do you want for dinner?" I asked.

I knew the answer, but I hoped he would say something different.

"Taco Bell!" Clayton said.

"Of course," I shook my head.

The boy loved Taco Bell, always ordering a chicken quesadilla and three soft tacos. That was his go-to every time I asked. Even though I could make a better quesadilla and tacos with my eyes closed, he always said he loved the sauce. That was the other thing he would do, get the hottest sauces and dump five packets all over it.

"So," Clayton said as we sat down to eat.

"I heard," I nodded.

"What do you think?" Clayton asked.

I shrugged and bit on my burrito.

"That bad huh?" Clayton asked.

I always thought if you had nothing good to say, keep your mouth shut. I did it, especially when it came down to Jacob and Alyssa, especially around Clayton.

"I know how you feel, and how they feel, so, it's best if I stay out of it," I nodded. "That okay?"

"Yeah," Clayton nodded. "Just wish you and Lisa would get along."

"Yeah, that's not going to happen," I said.

I didn't blame Alyssa for what happened, even though she hadn't been there, but I did blame her for getting with my husband. Friends didn't do that to each other.

"Change of subject," I said as I smiled at him.

Clayton was the spitting image of his father except for the dark black hair he got from me. Everything else was his father.

I took a playing card from my purse and pushed it to Clayton. "But Dad said I couldn't play any games because of my grades," Clayton beamed.

"I won't tell him if you don't," I said.

I had gotten a PS5 the moment they came out and were available. I knew how strict Jacob could be, so it was only fair that I would be the fun parent.

"I will have to use your account, so he doesn't see me online," Clayton said.

"Not a problem," I nodded.

Clayton's smile always made me feel better about things.

"You going to be, okay?" I asked.

Clayton was all smiles as he played his video game. I had to work a late shift at the bar, but I always alarmed the house, and Clayton was old enough to know never to answer the door.

I shook my head and went out the door.

"YOU NEED TO LET IT go," Kate said as we tended the bar together.

"I know," I nodded. "She's still a bitch!"

"You gave up the ability to call her anything the moment you sucked that cock," Kate said as she smiled at one of the guys.

"You keep saying that," I shook my head.

"Well, it's the truth," Kate said.

"You should have pulled me off him," I said, shaking my head as I cleaned a few glasses.

"Do we have to go over that night again?" Kate asked. "Every time you bring up Alyssa, we have to revisit that night, it's getting old!"

I lived in that night. When I went to sleep, it plagued me. Every time I looked at Jacob, I remembered the look on his face when he came through the door.

"You don't know what's it like," I shook my head.

"No, I don't," Kate said. "Because I can control myself when I drink."

I sighed as I looked at her. Kate was my best friend. "He's gone," Kate shrugged. "You have to accept that and move on."

Kate was always the voice of reason outside of my head. She was right about one thing. Jacob was gone. I could see it in his eyes. He was no longer interested in me other than the co-parent to his son.

I slowly opened the door to the house and crept inside. I smiled as I saw Clayton on the couch, all bundled up, with the headset still on his head. I turned off the television, armed the alarm, and headed to bed.

Another night spent alone, and another night I would dream of the man I could never have again.

Chapter Two: Trying to Get Ahead

After another night and another dream, I woke again to an empty bed. At least I had my son Clayton. I had a big day planned. He wanted to go to the water park.

I got changed, and we headed for the water park. As usual, during the summer, the place was jam-packed, wall-to-wall people, with kids running around like crazy.

It was fun watching Clayton run around and play with the others. That was the thing about Clayton. He never met a stranger. He was always making friends wherever he went.

It took hours to get Clayton out of the water and into the car so we could head home. He left with new friends to add to his growing number of friends online and on his video game systems.

'Crap,' I thought as I pulled up to the house.

Jesse was waiting for me, leaning against his truck. I had forgotten about him coming over to look over the deck.

"Go inside and get changed," I told Clayton as I pulled into the driveway.

"I took a look around," Jesse said as he approached me. "It doesn't look good."

I nodded, not wanting to open my mouth and say something I shouldn't. I knew Jesse was the one that told on me, I knew I shouldn't be mad at him because I was the one that did the cheating, but I was furious.

"So, there are a couple of options," Jesse said.

Again, I nodded as he started to go over the options. He, of course, started with the most expensive one, which I turned down immediately. The other two were just as bad. I agreed on the last one, it would take the most time, but it was the cheapest.

Jesse wrote it all up for me and handed me the paper. It would be one guy tearing it down, then rebuilding it himself. It would take a few weeks as he would do it in his spare time, but at least it would get done and cost me much less.

As Jesse was leaving, he turned to look at me. "You know," he said as he approached me again. "You can be mad at me all you want, you can also never talk to me again, but it wasn't me that sucked Johnny's cock in front of seven other people, while your best friend was shouting at you to stop, that wasn't me, that was all you!"

He turned around and headed for his truck. Jesse was right, and I knew it. I watched as his truck pulled away.

After the incident, I never saw Johnny again, although I did hear from him after I got divorced.

Johnny messaged me and asked if I wanted to meet him. I knew what he meant when he said he wanted to meet. He wanted more than to meet and talk. A lot of men did as soon as the news got out.

I was the talk of the bar and was sure of many other places. Guys would look at me with a smile or ask me for my number. Something they didn't do when I was married or before the incident. Even now, if someone talked about it, I would get looks.

Jesse's words stung for the rest of the day and into my night shift at the bar. I still remember everything that happened that night.

It wasn't like I blacked out or anything like that; I remember looking at Johnny with his tight abs and muscular chest. I remember him looking down at my bare chest and admiring the size of my tits.

We were flirting, and that's when it happened. Johnny just took his dick out. Instead of pushing him away or saying something, I, well, I did what I did.

I repeated that night many times inside my head but never came up with a clear-cut reason for doing it.

"Hey!" a voice said, breaking me out of my daydream and returning to the present.

"What?" I asked.

The guy ordered a drink, and I sighed as I made it.

The night was more of the same; guys ordered drinks, and I made them.

"So," one of the guys said as it was getting close to closing time.

"Nope," I replied.

"What was I going to say?" he asked.

"You were going to ask if you could take me home, or walk me to my car, or something along those lines," I said as I cleaned up. "And to all those thoughts, the answer is no."

"Unless your name is Johnny," another man said.

"Hank," I said as I looked at the man. "Haven't seen you around since."

"That night," Hank said as he sat down.

"We are closing," I said.

"One drink," Hank smiled.

"Okay," I nodded. I poured Hank a beer and set it down in front of him. "Just one."

"You look the same," Hank said as he looked at me.

"It hasn't been that long," I said, staring at him.

Hank was the friend that brought Johnny to the bar that night. I hadn't seen or heard from him since.

"So, what brings you back?" I asked. "Last I heard you got a nice gig out west somewhere."

"It was nice," Hank nodded. "But there is no place like home, right?"

"Uh-huh," I nodded.

Hank was always up to something. His mind was always working on an angle, something that either made him a decent amount of money or got him laid. I had known him since high school.

"Fine," Hank said as I kept staring at him. "I heard about your little problem, thought I could help out."

"My problem," I laughed. "What problem is that?"

"Your divorce, and I heard you haven't been with another man since," Hank smiled.

"That's none of your business," I said.

"Oh please, your girl toys must be working overtime," Hank said as he looked at the other man. "This woman right here, once took three guys and drained their balls, and still wanted more," Hank smiled.

I shook my head. "I was nineteen," I said. "That was a long time ago."

"How about Jason's party, on your twentieth?" Hank smiled. "Four guys that time," he nudged the guy. "Including yours truly."

"A lot of alcohol," I said, shaking my head. "And I mean a lot!"

"Or how about the night in question, that wasn't too long ago," Hank smiled. "Sucked my boys cock, right there in front of everyone," Hank shook his head. "The way your head just bobbed up and down, it was like looking at a professional, you didn't even stop to catch your breath."

"It wasn't that big," I said, shaking my head.

"Didn't stop you from slurping all that cum down, while he held your head down," Hank said, again looking at the man beside him. "He pushed her head down and held it down with both hands, you should have seen it!" Hank laughed. "My friend is built like a brickhouse and there he is using both hands and pushing her head down."

Hank even did the visual as if the other guy couldn't imagine what had happened.

"That's it," I said. I took the beer back and poured it down the sink. "You can go."

"I must have hit a nerve," Hank smiled as he got up. "If you change your mind, I am at the Quality down on fifth, next to the Waffle House," Hank said as he walked away.

I had no intention of visiting Hank. How dare he bring up the past like that? From high school to now, he has always been a pain in my side.

Hank knew how much I loved the jocks, with their muscular bodies, and, 'Dammit!,' I thought I was doing it again. "Casey, I am leaving, can you close up?" I said to my helper.

"Absolutely," Casey chimed as she came around the bar.

I sat in my car in the parking lot, trying to calm myself down. Everything Hank had said was true. The moment I turned eighteen, I turned into a complete slut, a whore, or whatever the guys called me.

For so long, I was cooped up in my house. My parents might have been drunk, high, or blitzed most of the time, but they kept me in my place throughout high school.

Straight to school and straight back home. They didn't want me to repeat what had happened with them; they never told me what had happened, but I could do the math, and it wasn't hard to figure out that they had me earlier than they wanted.

Sure, I kissed and made out with guys before, but nothing that pushed passed the boundaries and nothing under the clothes.

The very following night after my eighteenth birthday party. I sucked off four of the football players in the locker room of our school after we broke in to litter the place. After that night, everything was on the table.

I wanted to do it all. No holds barred. I had been face fucked, anal fucked, double and triple penetrated. My tits were fucked daily. Most of the guys. Especially Hank couldn't get enough of them. I was a cock whore, and I loved it.

Even through all of that, Jacob still flirted with me and treated me with high respect. Not once did he make a move on me. Even though he knew what was going on, he knew everything.

After that night in the woods, when I took Jacob's virginity, I settled down. The past came just that, the past.

I had never had a boyfriend before, not someone I would be loyal to, so it was hard initially. Jacob was fine with me flirting, but I never did anything with anyone else until that night.

I always tried to sum up why I did it and think of why I would betray Jacob's trust. Sex with Jacob was always mind-blowing good. He had a thick and long white cock that I loved. He would use toys on me anytime I wanted and always ensured I was satisfied.

I tried to blame it on him traveling a lot, but that wasn't the reason, either. The moment he came home, he made every day he was home about Clayton and me.

The simple reason was I made the wrong decision. Since then, I quit drinking; I wasn't like some people who drank to take the edge of the day away; no, I was just like my parents. I drank and drank until I was completely and utterly blitzed.

Hank knew my weakness, I would be infatuated with Johnny's colossal biceps and bulging muscles, and I loved the attention my large breasts brought me. He had set me up.

Hank always picked on Jacob in high school. The two had a rivalry that still carries on to this day. I didn't know how it started but I knew it wouldn't end.

When Hank got the job at the supermarket, Jacob made sure to visit every day, go down Hank's aisle, and drop or break things so that Hank would have to clean them up.

Then they became adults, and things spiraled out of control. Jacob always flaunted that he made a lot more than Hank. Jacob had a lovely house, excellent vehicles, and a busty wife, while Hank lived paycheck to paycheck and rented a small apartment alone.

I would have blamed Hank for telling Jacob what happened that night, but they didn't talk to each other.

"I knew you would come by," Hank said as I knocked on his door.

"Shut up," I said as I pushed past him and entered the small hotel room.

"You told Jesse to tell Jacob," I said as I spun around and confronted him.

"Guilty as charged," Hank said, closing the door and lighting a cigarette.

The small no-smoking sign was on the table as he sat down.

That was Hank. From the day he was born, he never followed the rules, even his parent's rules.

They were killed in a house fire when Hank was seventeen. Many people thought Hank was the one that set the fire, but he was out on the town with his friends when everything happened, and all evidence pointed to one of his parents having a cigarette in bed.

I remembered that night when they told Hank his parents were dead. He didn't even shed a tear.

"Why?" I asked.

"Why not?" Hank shrugged.

"It had nothing to do with you," I shook my head.

"Not the way I see it," Hank said as he stared at my tits. "Your husband was always pushing the limit of my patience, always flaunting his new truck or how he could come to my shop and buy things I couldn't dream of buying."

"So, that's why you brought your friend," I nodded.

"I know you like the back of my hand," Hank shook his head with a smile. "You try and play the good housewife, but deep down, you're nothing but the same whore that fucked me and my friends for a ride to the concert."

I shook my head. "I was a damned good wife, and a good mother!"

"A good wife, wouldn't have jumped in the pool topless, a good mother wouldn't have been there in the first place, so get off that high horse!" Hank yelled. "A good mother would have gone home after closing and been with her son!"

I reached forward and slapped Hank as hard as I could.

Hank smiled. "A good wife wouldn't have sucked another man's cock!" he said as he wiped the blood from his lip.

I rushed for the door, but Hank barred the way. "A good woman wouldn't come all this way, just to tell me off," Hank said as he pinned me against the wall.

"Shut up," I said as he kissed me.

I started kissing him back as he flung me onto the small bed. He tore at my jeans and underwear as he pushed himself into me.

I felt his stiff cock enter me as he thrust deep inside me. "I knew you were still a whore!" Hank said as he started to fuck me.

"Shut up," I said as I wrapped my legs around him, pulling him onto me.

I wanted to be fucked, to push that memory of that night away, make it go away deep inside of me, just like Hank's cock was doing now.

"Fuck," Hank said as he continued to thrust into me. With each thrust, I felt his body quiver on top of me.

I gripped his cock tight. I wanted to feel anything other than my empty feelings for the past two years.

"Look at me!" Hank said, gripping my neck and twisting my face towards his face.

He loved watching his women as he came inside of them.

I felt his cock throb as he shot his load into me. I pushed him off me as soon as he was done. I gripped my jeans and pulled them up and buckled the button.

"Come back when you want another fix," Hank said as he lit another cigarette as he laid out on the bed.

I slammed the door behind me.

"Of course," I said as I looked at my car. It had started to rain.

I slowly walked towards my car.

"PLEASE TELL ME YOU didn't go with him?" Kate asked.

"Who?" I asked as I watched Clayton and Darold aim and fire their bows at the targets.

We had gone to an outdoor range so they could get used to firing their bows in the elements instead of always being at the indoor range.

Darold was Kate's son. He was ten. Clayton and Darold had been best friends as soon as they could walk. Usually, where you found one, the other wasn't too far behind.

"Don't," Kate said.

I nodded. She must have heard that Hank had been in the bar.

"It's not like that," I said.

"That man has had you wrapped around his finger since day one," Kate said.

"I think that goes both ways," I replied.

"Oh really?" Kate said as she stared at me. "Tell me you didn't fuck him last night?"

I shook my head and turned my attention back to our kids.

"Thought as much," Kate said as she looked at me.

"It wasn't anything," I said. "I just wanted to clear my head and I always think more clearly after having sex."

"Right," Kate nodded.

Kate knew me very well. She knew I was telling her the half-truth. Hank had always had a way of getting what he wanted from me when he wanted it.

Except for the few years I was married to Jacob. That was the real reason he was back in town.

"You know he is only here to get you," Kate said.

"Well, that's not going to happen," I shook my head. "He's not that good."

Hank wasn't good at all. He was a good fuck, but not anything I would marry or even want to keep around as a long-term fuck buddy.

"It's still going to the left," Clayton said as he brought his bow.

I looked at it, took my tools out, and played with the alignment. The only good thing about me sleeping around with many guys was I learned much of everything.

I never really went to the mechanics, except for anything major, as I could do most of the minor things. I could go hunting and fishing, and I knew how to throw and take a punch.

"Try now," I said.

There was a time after Clayton was born when Hank told everyone that Clayton was his child. I knew from the moment I saw Clayton that he was Jacob's son, same blue eyes, same cheekbones, and the same look when Clayton's eyes looked at me.

Hank wanted it so badly that he kept asking for a blood test, so we gave it to him. Clayton was Jacob's son, without a shadow of a doubt.

"Thanks Mom!" Clayton yelled from the range.

I waved back at him.

"What if he comes around?" Kate asked.

"Hank's slow on the uptake, but he knows when not to push the boundaries," I nodded. "I already warned him I have no problems shooting him if he comes near Clayton."

"That I don't doubt," Kate smiled.

After we finished at the range, I took them to eat at their favorite place, and then I had to drop Clayton off. It was always painful when I made the drop.

Clayton ran out and hugged Alyssa, and then they went inside. Jacob walked up to my car. "I heard Hank is back in town."

"I can handle it," I nodded.

"What's he after?" Jacob asked.

"The usual," I shrugged.

"You're not going to give in to him, right?" Jacob asked.

"What did you say to me, when I asked about Alyssa moving in with you?" I asked as I looked at him. "That's right," I nodded. "The best thing about divorce is you don't get to ask questions."

I pulled away and didn't look back.

'Maybe having Hank back in town wasn't a bad thing after all,' I thought as I drove home.

Chapter Three: Down the fox hole

"Are you okay?" Charles asked as he came into my office. "Yeah," I responded.

"Just that you gave me this report twice," Charles said, dropping a yellow folder on my desk.

"Shit," I said as I got the correct report and handed it to him.

"What's going on?" Charles asked.

"I hate that everyone thinks this is a small town," I said, shaking my head. "Always in everyone else's business. When they should stay in their own fucking lanes!"

Charles nodded as he sat down across from me.

"It might not be a small town, but most of us, hang out at the same bar, our kids go to some of the same schools, and the same grocery stores, it's only natural that some people form a tight knit community."

"Well, they can go join another community, and stay the hell out of mine," I said.

"Hank, huh?" Charles asked.

"You heard," I said.

"Hard not to, the guy is a walking time bomb," Charles shook his head.

Hank was just that. No one knew when he would blow up on someone or do something stupid.

One day in high school, he climbed to the roof to write that he loved Jessica Tolban in dark black on the white wall.

Another time he jumped off the water tower into the river on a dare. He had broken more bones than anyone I know for the dumbest reasons.

"You keep clear of him," Charles said as he stood up. "I know you both have a history, but some people were born trouble, and he is one of them."

I nodded as he left my office. I knew everyone was right, but Hank always was the person that wasn't easy to stay away from, he had ways of getting under my skin, and as much as I didn't want to scratch it, I just had to do it.

"SO, THIS IS WHERE YOU live?" Hank asked as I pulled up to my house.

I moved out of the other house as soon as we divorced. I had moved so that I was closer to Clayton.

"What do you want?" I asked as I got out of my car. "I have had a long day at work, and I just want to soak in a bath," I said as I walked toward my house.

Hank got off his large bike and walked toward me. "Not going to invite me in?" he asked.

"No," I shook my head. "The other night was just that, a quick fuck and now I am over it."

"Really?" Hank smiled.

He had more gray in his long beard than black, and his head showed signs of him balding in the middle. Hank had always been reckless, which showed in his face, arms, and hands. He had scars everywhere.

From bar fights to reckless stunts, he had done it all. All it took was someone to dare him to do something, and he would do it.

"Yes, really," I said as I turned to face him. "Look I am going to say this one more time, and maybe you will get it through that thick head," I said as I stood my ground. "Whatever we had in high school and everything that followed was in the past, and that's where it is going to stay, do I make myself clear?"

"Your mouth says that," Hank smiled as he walked closer to me.

"No, all of me says that, the other night, was just that one night. It will not happen again," I shook my head.

I put my hand behind me to grip my pistol. Hank stopped in his tracks.

"You know how good a shot I am," I nodded. "Now kindly leave."

Hank smiled and nodded. "We will talk again," he said as he walked towards his bike.

The loud bike started and then took off down the road.

I watched to make sure he was genuinely gone before entering the house. I made sure everything was locked and then armed the alarm.

Hank never liked taking no for an answer, and it would be like him to return.

I soaked in the tub and relaxed.

"What are you going to do?" Kate asked.

"Nothing," I replied.

I was sipping on my sweet tea, something I had started after that night. I pretended it had more than just tea in it. I didn't drink at home, in case I went too far and decided to call someone or go somewhere I shouldn't. I was trying to make better decisions for myself.

'Where was that thought, the other night?' I thought to myself.

"What if he comes back around?" Kate asked.

I was sitting on my couch and talking to Kate on the phone. She continuously checked on me and ensured I was where I was supposed to be. She was like a sister to me.

"I will have a surprise waiting for him," I said as I eyed my gun on the table. I had more than one. A few were lying around in strategic positions.

"Good," Kate replied.

"The alarm is on, and I am sure he is at the bar, damaging his kidneys even more," I said.

"Well, if you need anything, call me, or text me," Kate said.

"You too, just in case," I said.

"He isn't that stupid," Kate said.

I shook my head, Hank was a pain in the ass, but he knew who not to mess with, and Kate was one of them. I thought I had more than enough protection for my house.

Kate's house was a fortress. She lived out in the boonies, away from all of us. It was a good thirty-minute drive to her house, most of it through back roads.

Kate had trip wire, barbed wire, and other things around her house. No one was that stupid.

It all stemmed from her last boyfriend. The guy turned into a total stalker after they broke up. She found him standing in her bedroom, staring down at her one night.

How he got in was a total mystery, as the alarm was set, and he hadn't broken anything. The cop's going theory was that he had snuck in when the alarm was off and stayed quiet in another room or the attic.

After that night, Kate went total commando, looking up things she could make or buy that would fortify the house.

Luckily Darold wasn't home, or she would have killed him. She had beaten him severely and hadn't seen him since, but occasionally, she would look around as if she caught a glimpse of him.

Darold's father was a sperm donor, as we called him. It was a one-night fling that resulted in Kate becoming pregnant.

Of course, when she came and told him about it, he acted like it was the best thing that could happen to them, but less than a week later, he was gone. He packed up his house, left his job, and was nowhere to be found.

Kate could have gone after him legally for support, but she was an independent woman. She always said it took two to make a baby, and she was just as fault as he was. As Kate said, she spread her legs and invited him in. Even though they used protection, the result was Darold.

I was his godmother, and I loved the kid. He was shy at times, which made me smile as he hardly looked people in the eye, always holding his head down.

Clayton was the one that got them into trouble, doing things they shouldn't. After an incident at the gas station, I had to talk with Clayton and told him there were certain things he could do that Darold would get in serious trouble for; at first, he didn't understand; Darold was his best friend, but Clayton didn't see the color difference.

Darold was half white and half black. While he was lightly colored, many people only saw the black in him.

One day Clayton came home and said he understood what I had said. He told me they were at a store buying clothes with Alyssa, and the lady at the store kept looking at Darold rudely, as Clayton said, and she asked Alyssa for Darold to keep his hands out of his pockets and take down the hoodie.

Alyssa was furious as Clayton was wearing the same exact hoodie and had it up and had his hands in his pockets, just like Darold. From that day forward, Clayton always looked after his friend.

"Well," I said.

I got up from the couch and went upstairs. It was another night, and I was sure I would have that same dream again.

I went online to chat with some of my faraway friends. We talked for a bit, and after a while, I got bored and was about to close my laptop.

Then I decided to read a few stories. I loved reading erotic stories before going to bed. It was something I had picked up after the divorce.

I logged in and found a new story by one of the authors I followed. Reading the story got me all hot, and as usual, I went down to leave her a comment.

I sighed as I saw the usual anonymous comments.

"Fucking keyboard warriors," I sighed as I typed a response to one of them.

My author loved writing stories that pushed the boundaries. This story was about a female having sex with her boss behind her husband's back at the company's party.

Of course, some saw fit to call her out on it. Wishing death on the cheating woman or worse. When the author wrote a story about a man cheating on his wife, none of them said anything. Not one single word about how it was terrible for him to cheat on his wife. Not a single comment that he should die or catch something.

These people were the same ones that went into the interracial section and downvoted or plagued the comments with racial slurs or comments. The worst thing was they hit the little coward button, making sure to comment under an anonymous name to shield themselves from reprisal.

'Fucking cowards!' I thought.

Why didn't they stay away if they didn't like the story? It was like going into a Mexican restaurant, knowing you don't like Mexican food.

After several rounds of going back and forth, I decided it was a lost cause and settled into my bed.

"Dammit," I said as I knew I couldn't sleep.

I reached under my bed and grabbed my colossal toy chest. Jacob always laughed when I went for it.

"Why does it have to be so big?" he asked the first night.

Then I opened it. His eyes went huge. I bought a lot of toys for myself over the years. More than any sane woman should have, I always thought.

I got down on my knees and looked through the various toys. I had everything anyone would need and more. There was another one like it in the walk-in closet.

"Ah!" I said, reaching for the one I wanted to use tonight.

It was a mold of Jacob's cock. I had sent it to my favorite website, and they made it so that I could press the button, and fake liquid cum would shoot out the tip.

I pushed my chest back under my bed and looked online for my favorite porn. I found it and slid the large dildo into me.

I slowly worked it into me until it was deep inside, and then I pushed the laptop away. I imagined it was Jacob. He always went slow at first. Sometimes he would go slow throughout, and then there were times he would fuck me so hard it felt like he would break the bed.

I was going for the slow and steady. I loved it when Jacob did that. He would look down at me like I was the only woman on earth.

I could feel the tension building in my stomach, and I started to arch my back. I stopped going slow and started fucking myself with it, furiously pushing it in and out of me. It was building inside of me. That's when I pushed the button.

Jacob loved cumming inside me from when I got pregnant to the last time. He loved cumming inside, calling me his cum dumpster or cum slut. I had to beg him a couple of times to cum on my tits or my face. Even when he tit fucked me, he would grab my head and push his cock into my mouth.

"I don't want to waste it," Jacob often said.

"Cum inside me, Jacob," I yelled as I felt the liquid shoot into me.

After I came down and my breathing stopped, I knew that would never happen again. Jacob and his colossal cock belonged to someone else.

He was cumming inside her now, calling her his cum slut and whore.

I dropped the toy to the floor and then turned on my side as I fell asleep alone.

Chapter Four: Open Minds

"What the hell?" I said as my phone chirped as I was sitting at my desk at work.

It was a notification from my alarm app that someone was at my house. I looked at the camera view and saw a black man walking up to my front door. I hadn't ordered anything,

"Can I help you?" I asked through the talk button of the app as he got closer to the door.

"Jesse sent me to do your deck," the man said. "Name's Andrew."

Jesse never gave me a name. He just said someone would be coming around. "Hold on," I said.

"Be right here," Andrew replied.

I texted Jacob to ask Jesse about the guy at my door. I didn't have Jesse's number, and I didn't want it.

'All good. Jesse said he's the person,' Jacob texted me quickly.

He must have been near Jesse, or Jesse was at their house.

"Fine," I said.

"Okay, I will get started," Andrew said.

I turned the view to the back camera and saw Andrew, with his tools starting to tear down the deck.

"What's going on?" Charles asked as he looked at my phone.

"The guy is taking down the deck," I said.

"Ah, Andrew!" Charles said.

"You know him?" I asked.

"Yeah, he did some great work in our backyard. He gave us a barbecue pit and a stone fire stove. It was great work," Charles said. "Took him a while, but it was well worth it."

I nodded and set my phone on the desk to see what he was doing.

"You've got that look," Charles said as he stared down at me.

"What look?" I asked.

"You know very well what look, what's on your mind," Charles said as he sat down.

"It's nothing, just thinking about my parents," I said.

Charles knew my parents very well. He had gone to school with them; he was practically my godfather, so I often confided in him.

"Ah," Charles said. "They would have a fit," he smiled.

To say my parents were racist was like saying water was wet. I heard more names for other ethnic groups come out of their mouths than I heard my name.

"Glad you're not like that," Charles said.

I was for a long time. I always made racial jokes or snide comments. That was until Darold was born. All of that changed the moment I held that baby in my arms. His tiny hand gripped my finger, and everything I thought vanished at that moment.

Sure, I slipped now and then, but I was a changed person for the most part.

"NO, THE FUCK YOU'RE not!" Kate said as she laughed at me.

"I am!" I said as we talked on the phone during my lunch break.

"Excuse me," Kate said. "How about the time the guy cut you off when we went to the restaurant, two weeks ago?"

"I didn't mean it," I said, shaking my head. I had called him the N-word, but I was angry, and he had cut me off.

"The Chinese guy at the restaurant?" Kate asked.

"It's only polite to talk in English, when someone asks you a question," I shrugged.

"We were in a Chinese restaurant!" Kate said. "And he was talking to one of the other staff members."

"In America!" I replied. "And I was the one that asked the question!"

Kate said several times that I had gone off the rails as she would say.

"I just have different views, they aren't that bad," I said.

"You have an opinion," Kate corrected me. "Anyone you don't know completely is bad and will stay on your alert list until they prove otherwise," Kate nodded.

"Doesn't everyone do that?" I asked.

"Yes, and no," Kate said. "Most of us do it for everyone. You do it with most ethnic groups," Katie sighed.

"I do not," I said.

"Who is Clayton interested in, right now?" Katie asked.

"Easy the blonde girl in his school with the curly hair," I nodded.

"Wrong," Kate said. "Try again."

"No," I said, remembering he pointed her out a few times. "She's the short girl with the curly blonde hair. She wears a lot of yellow."

"Nope," Kate said.

I got angry and video-called her. She answered, and I saw that she was in her office at the residential home.

"What are you talking about?" I asked. "He pointed to her, and said she was cute," I said.

"Yes, that's Shelly, Nick and Danelle's girl, but no, he isn't interested in her. Clayton told me he pointed her out to you because you asked why he was smiling all the time," Kate said.

"Okay, so who is it?" I asked.

"Hispanic girl, named Helena," Katie said.

"What?" I asked. "Who the fuck is Helena?"

"See," Katie said.

"No, nothing to do with her being Hispanic or whatever, I don't know who she is," I said.

"Long black hair, wears jeans, and is always near your son," Kate said.

"Doesn't ring a bell," I said. "Wait," I said as I remembered a girl at the water park. "Her hair is really dark black, like oily black. Taller than Clayton?"

"That's her," Kate nodded.

"Why didn't he tell me?" I asked.

"Alyssa was the one that told me, then he told me afterward," Kate said.

"Alyssa knows?" I shouted.

"You should be asking Clayton, why he is scared to tell you," Katie said.

I felt a pit in my stomach for the rest of the day. My son was scared to tell me something. That didn't sit right with me at all.

'Can I pick up Clayton from school?' I texted Jacob.

'Have to ask Alyssa, she is taking him to football practice,' Jacob replied.

'Fuck me,' I thought as I scrolled to Alyssa's name.

'Can I pick up Clayton? I need to talk to him. I can bring him to the field,' I sent.

'Sure, I will pick up his gear and meet you there,' Alyssa replied.

No doubt Jacob had talked to her first, or she would have said something else.

I left work early and waited in the long line of cars to pick up the kids. I saw Clayton and Darold. Sure enough, there she was a tall Hispanic girl with them. She was there with a black girl. All four of them were talking and smiling.

When I pulled up, the two girls looked like they had seen a ghost and took off.

"Where's Alyssa?" Clayton said as he climbed into the back seat. Darold waved at us as I drove off. I knew Kate's mother was picking him up as usual.

"I needed to talk to you," I said as I watched him buckle his seat belt.

"Okay," Clayton nodded.

"So, who's the two girls?" I asked.

"Just some friends," Clayton said.

"Clayton," I said in my stern voice. "Who are the two girls?"

"You're just going to get mad," Clayton replied.

"I will get even more mad if you don't tell me," I said, looking back at him.

"Jessica and Helena," Clayton sighed.

"Friends?" I asked.

"Yes," Clayton said with a smile.

I smiled back at him. "See not mad," I said. "Which one do you like?" I asked.

"Helena," Clayton said with an even bigger smile.

I knew it was the usual innocent girl/boy crushes at this stage. She probably did something he liked, or they both enjoyed each other's company.

"The dark haired one?" I asked.

"Yes," Clayton nodded. "Darold likes Jessica," he said.

I nodded. "See, not that hard," I shrugged.

"Didn't know how you would take it," Clayton said.

I pulled the car over and looked back at him. "There is nothing you can say that will make me mad at you, do you understand?"

Clayton nodded.

"Nothing, as long as it's the truth, I will stand right beside you," I told him.

"It's just that I know how grandpa and grandma were, and I thought you would be the same," Clayton admitted.

"Well, they are both dead and buried," I said as I pulled the car back onto the road. "And I am nothing like them."

I dropped Clayton off at the field and waved at Alyssa as I pulled away.

"It's understandable," Kate said as I went to her house.

Darold was outside playing with their dog while we talked on the deck.

"How so?" I asked.

"You were like them for a while," Kate said.

"I was not as bad as them," I said.

"You have said some pretty bad things about many people of color," Katie said. "And don't forget how you reacted when I told you that Darold's father was a black guy."

"I didn't react that badly," I said.

"You said it was typical, and that they are all like that," Katie said.

"Well, I wasn't wrong," I replied.

"Oh really?" Kate said. "How many kids does Hank have and take care of?"

"Hank is Hank," I shrugged. "Any woman that...."

I stopped as she looked at me. "Got me there," I nodded.

Hank had at least four kids that I knew of, and as I knew, he liked to go anywhere and everywhere on his bike. I was sure there were many more out there. Hank hated using protection, and he never pulled out.

"Okay, I was about to say it's okay for him to do it, but no one else," Katie said. "What about Jeff?"

"You made your point," I said, shaking my head.

Jeff was the owner of the bar. He had cheated on Alice, his now ex-wife. Jeff bounced when the mistress announced she was pregnant, leaving them both high and dry. He ran things through his brother Trevor.

"Okay, because I can say at least four more names, if you want me to?" Katie said.

"No, it's okay," I nodded my defeat.

"There are a lot of men and women of all ethnicity and backgrounds that leave their kids. If they all stayed and were actual parents, there would be fewer kids in foster care," Kate said.

"But doesn't it make you mad?" I asked. "Darold is his kid?"

"Why should he have stayed?" Kate asked. "We weren't dating. We weren't serious. It was a second date that went too far. We had a lot to drink, and things got carried away. We used protection, and it happened, end of the story."

I looked at her. She said it so simply.

"What?" Kate asked.

"Nothing," I shook my head.

"Why did I date a black guy?" Kate asked. "You've had that look on your face every time we talk about it."

"None of my business," I shook my head.

"He had a super big black cock. It was fourteen inches long and as thick as a baseball bat," Kate said as she looked at me.

"Stop it," I said.

"No, that's what you want to hear or think, right?" Kate said. "When he took his big black cock out of his pants, I couldn't help myself. I had to drop to my lily-white knees and suck it dry."

"Now, you're just being stupid," I said, shaking my head.

"The sex was awesome. He went all night, never stopping, and when he came, it was so much it could fill three large buckets," Kate laughed.

"Now you sound like some of those porn stories," I laughed with her.

"Hey, that's what they believe and comment on, right?" Kate shrugged.

"Then they are stupid and should be taken out back and put down like that dog," I said, shaking my head. "They are just made-up stories. If they want to believe that it's all true, I am going to my house, getting my lightsaber, and using the force to get Jacob back."

Kate spat out her sweet tea as she looked at me.

"I am serious, I am going to hop in my starship, go to warp speed, use the force, and get Jacob back from that evil witch of the west," I smiled.

We both laughed at it all.

"Why did you?" I asked.

"He was a nice guy," Kate shrugged. "Plain and simple, he treated me nice, and we talked for a long time before our first date. The sex was just that sex, just like any other male out there. No different, good or bad, and if I had to do it all again, I would."

I looked down at the result, a young boy playing tug of war with his dog.

"I wouldn't and don't blame you," I said, looking at my friend. "You know that right?"

Kate nodded.

WHILE DRIVING HOME, I thought about the things we had talked about, things I thought I had put out of my head.

I used to be one of those that said things like what was happening to Darold never happened, and it was fake news and fake media. And that people were blowing things out of proportion.

That was until I held that little baby in my arms, and he looked up at me with those dark brown eyes and held my finger. That's when the what-ifs came into my head. No one thinks of those things until they are put into that situation.

The first time I saw an elderly lady grab her purse as if her life depended on it when we were in McDonald's because Darold stood close to her to order his food, it made me so mad I wanted to punch her in her AARP face, but then it dawned on me.

How many times had I done that? How many times inadvertently had I done something like that? She didn't know Darold was the sweetest kid in the world.

After that day, things changed. I started to see reactions everywhere. Darold, like Clayton, loved wearing hoodies. Whether it was hot as hell outside or cold as the tundra, they both wore hoodies.

'Where are you?' Jacob texted me as I pulled into the driveway.

'Home,' I replied.

'Need to talk to you, heading over,' he said.

Andrew came from behind the house as I pulled in. He walked toward me.

I saw him for the first time. He was a tall man, easily taller than my five-nine frame. He towered over me, which didn't happen often.

"I took down the deck, and put some wood up to bar the door, so it won't open," Andrew said as he met me.

"Thanks," I said, staring up at him.

I wasn't used to staring up at most men; usually, I stood close to their height. Jacob was five-eleven, and Hank was shorter than me at five-eight, so this was new territory, the tallest man I knew was Tanner at the bowling alley, and he was six-three. Andrew stood taller than him.

He wasn't just tall. He was broad, with bulging muscles, and when he smiled, it almost looked out of place for such a huge man.

We walked around the back, and my deck was gone. There was no sign of it.

"Where's all the pieces or the wood?" I asked.

"I took some of it to the dump, as well as gave some of it away," Andrew said. "People like to use the wood for their pits."

I nodded.

"Jesse ordered everything so as soon as it shows up, I will be back to put it back together again," Andrew said.

"Good," I nodded.

"If there is anything else," Andrew said as he gave me a card. "Just call me."

"Actually," I said. "I don't know if you can do it, but the fan in my bedroom hasn't worked in months."

"Ceiling?" Andrew asked.

"Yeah," I nodded as we walked back to the front.

Jacob had just pulled up as we started walking inside.

"Hey Andrew," Jacob said as he walked inside with us.

"Jacob," Andrew nodded.

"Having him look at the ceiling fan?" Jacob asked.

"Yeah, since no one else will look at it," I said.

"People have been busy," Jacob replied.

"No such thing," Andrew retaliated.

I smiled. "I like you," I laughed as I looked at Andrew.

"Too many people are using that bullshit excuse these days," Andrew said. "There are twenty-four hours in a day. If you sleep eight of those hours, it still leaves sixteen. If you work a full twelve-hour shift, it still leaves four. How the hell are you that busy? Even with kids and activities, it takes less than a minute to text or call someone to tell them hi or ask what's going on. What stops you from doing any of those? People use busy as an excuse, not a reason."

"Not many people work a full twelve-hour shift without breaks, or lunches," I said as I led him into the bedroom.

"Or sleep for eight hours straight, even when they lie down to go to bed, they have their phones in their faces," Andrew said. "Like I said, complete bullshit."

"I will wait out here," Jacob said, shaking his head as he stood in the living room.

I flicked the switch and pulled on the chains, and nothing happened.

Andrew looked at it and nodded. "Let me get my tools, and I will take a look at it."

I went back out to Jacob and sat down.

"Clayton told me you guys talked," Jacob said.

"Yeah, we did," I nodded.

"Surprised," Jacob said.

"Why is everyone surprised?" I shook my head. "A person can change."

"I know, but you were always so," Jacob stopped as he thought.

"Don't say it," I shook my head.

I hated the word racist. It wasn't racism, more like prejudice, I had views and thoughts, and now I realized some were far-fetched and borderline wrong in some cases.

"Okay, I won't," Jacob nodded.

Jacob was what some of my old friends would call far left. I had been right-minded, not far right, just on the right side of the middle. Now I was squarely in the middle, just like Kate.

"Just to let you know," Jacob said. "I wanted to tell you, but Clayton made me promise not to," he said.

"It's alright," I nodded. "We talked, he thought I would be like my parents, and I am not."

During our marriage, we promised each other not to bring up our political or religious views. When voting came about, we voted separately, and we both weren't big television watchers, so the news or media never came up.

We raised Clayton to make up his own mind, never telling him how he should think or feel. We decided to let him form his opinions of the world around him.

I was glad he was becoming more like me than his father.

We heard Andrew working in my bedroom, and while Jacob turned to look at the hallways, I snuck a look at his crotch.

I thought about how I missed that huge white cock. I looked away as he turned back to me.

"So, everything is good?" Jacob asked as he stared at his phone.

No doubt the bitch was texting him and asking where he was. She was like that, always wondering where he was, who he was with, and when he would be home.

Jacob didn't have to worry about her. The bitch ran a predictable schedule. She worked down at the physical therapy clinic, packed a lunch so she didn't have to leave work, picked Clayton up from school, went running for ten miles at four in the afternoon, came home, made dinner, watched reality television, then went to bed, rinse and repeat.

Alyssa even had an app that calculated the carbs and calories everyone ate daily. I told her to turn that shit off while I had Clayton. I wouldn't follow no app's advice on feeding my son. If he wanted the whole menu from Taco Bell, he wasn't getting the entire fucking menu.

"You better go, before she has a conniption," I said with a smile.

"Yeah," Jacob said as he stood up.

I smiled as he stood up. He had a chubby. No doubt he had been staring at my cleavage. He did love my big boobs. How he went from someone with extremely large breasts to a flat-chested bitch boggled my mind.

"Hope she takes care of that," I smiled as he walked towards the door.

"She does," Jacob said. "And I don't have to worry about her sucking another guys cock," he said as he looked back at me as he held the door open. "Any other smart comments?"

"Nope," I said as he had won the argument.

"Good," Jacob said as he went out the door.

"Fucking stupid bitch," I cursed myself for saying that to him.

"It's working," Andrew said, startling me as I had completely forgotten he was here.

"Great," I said, standing up and following him into the bedroom.

The ceiling fan was spinning, and the light was on. I smiled and looked up at him. "How much do I owe you?" I asked.

"Nothing," Andrew smiled. "It was an easy fix."

I had to smile back at him. I knew from his height; that he was getting a good view of my cleavage.

"Just let me know if there is anything else," Andrew said as I walked him out.

"Make sure to lock up," Andrew said as he walked toward his truck.

"Definitely," I nodded as I stood at my doorstep.

I watched as his truck pulled out of the driveway, and he honked the horn as he left. I smiled and waved at him.

Then my face dropped as I saw Hank a few houses down. He was on his bike and staring directly at me. I shook my head and then closed the door.

I made sure everything was locked and then armed the alarm. I peeked out of my bedroom window, and Hank was still there.

'Hank is outside my house, a few doors down,' I texted Charles.

'I will handle it,' Charles responded.

Charles was the closest to me. I knew if I told Jacob, he would call the police, which would anger Hank more than needed.

I looked again and saw Charles's truck next to Hank's bike. They seemed to be talking for a while; then Hank took off like a bat from hell.

'Handled,' Charles replied.

I settled back into bed and thought about things other than Hank and his crush on me. Namely, Jacob and his cock.

"Stupid bitch," I said as I grabbed my pillow.

Chapter Five: Letting it All Out.

"Just great," I said as I pulled into work. Hank was waiting for me inside the parking lot.

As I parked, he started heading over to me.

He wouldn't be stupid to try something with all my co-workers standing around, so I got out of the car and stared at him as he walked toward me.

"What?" I asked.

"Now, you're fucking," he stopped as he saw some of the black males from my job standing at the loading dock.

"Go ahead," I said with a smile. "Say it, I dare you," I said as I looked at him.

"You know what I was going to say," Hank shook his head.

"No, I don't, I want you to say it loud and proud," I smiled as I looked at him.

Again, he looked at the loading dock, then shook his head. Hank was many things suicidal wasn't one of them.

"You're the one that came here, I didn't invite you," I said as I got my things out of my car. "You have something to say, then say it, or get the fuck gone."

"If I knew you liked those kinds, I would have never allowed you in my hotel room," Hank said.

"You're still on that?" I laughed. "It wasn't that big of a deal; I have watched commercials that have lasted longer."

Hank stepped closer to me as I challenged his manhood.

"What? You don't like the truth?" I said, shaking my head. "You are losing your touch."

There was a time when Hank could fuck me into exhaustion, and I was sure those days were way behind him. He had a beer gut and even standing here in the sun. I could see he was breathing heavily.

"Fuck you," Hank shook his head. "I tried to come back here and help you out, but you know what, you're not worth it!"

Hank walked away and headed for his bike. "Enjoy your colored boyfriend," he said as he started his motorcycle.

I didn't have it in me to tell him that Andrew was just someone doing work around the house. If he wanted to believe I was fucking Andrew, that was on him.

"Bye," I waved as he roared out of the parking lot.

"So, you're sleeping with a brother," Logan asked as I walked into the office through the loading dock.

"You wish," I smiled.

Logan and the other dock workers were harmless. Even if Hank said the word, they would probably yell at him or tell him off, but none of them would hurt him.

As for me, they were my co-workers, sure they would call me names and whistle at me, but not one of them made a serious move on me, even after the divorce.

My favorite was Ms. New Booty. I had to listen to the song to get the meaning, but the name fitted me, so I let them keep calling me it.

"One day that ass is going to have a brother hitting it from behind, mark my words," Johnathan said.

"Only when he is dreaming," I smiled as I went to my office.

I had nothing against interracial dating or relationships for everyone else. It wasn't for me, not that I didn't find some males of different ethnicities attractive.

I couldn't see myself with someone I didn't have a lot of things in common with, and for the most part, none of the guys I had met so far clicked on my level.

Sure, coming from the woman that fucked four guys on a whim all at once in every imaginable way possible until all of us were laid out all over the place exhausted was hypocritical. Okay, it was totally hypocritical, but that part of me was long gone.

I wanted something like I had with Jacob that meant the world to me. I wanted someone that woke up every day and thought of me. And before they went to bed, they wished I was in bed with them. I didn't want to just fuck and not be with that someone romantically anymore.

When I was Jacob, I had all of that; he was the first person I thought about when I woke up and the last person I thought about when I went to bed. We would text or call each other daily, and even though he worked hard and was out of town, he got a message from me throughout the day.

Sometimes I even sent him pictures of me. Nothing too wrong, but a photo showing my cleavage or a new bra I had bought, or if I thought my jeans looked good on my ass.

Even if I was having a good hair day or my nails looked good, Jacob was the first to get a picture, reminding him how much I loved him, and it was my way of letting him know I was thinking about him.

I wasn't like some of the other basic bitches online that took pictures they sent to everyone or posted them on their timelines or online for the whole world to see.

I took different pictures for my social pages and images that only Jacob got and no one else. That's what I wanted, no more fucking around, no more doing things on impulse.

I had that one night with Hank because I needed to think clearly, and I was hoping he would accept that it was a one-time thing.

"Thanks again for last night," I told Charles as he popped into my office.

"No problem," Charles responded. "He pulls that shit again, just let me know."

I nodded as I went deep into my work, putting Hank out of my head.

'We need to talk,' Jacob texted me just after lunch.

'Okay, can it wait, or do you want me to call you?' I replied.

'It can wait, meet me at your bar, after work,' Jacob said.

I agreed and wondered what it was about. Hopefully, he still wasn't mad about my stupid comment last night before he left the house.

I hurried to the bar after work and saw Jacob sitting in his usual booth in the corner.

"Thought you were off today?" Trevor asked.

"I am," I said as I headed for the booth.

"I ordered mozzarella sticks for you," Jacob said as I sat down.

"Oh no," I said, shaking my head.

I loved mozzarella sticks. They were my favorite appetizers. The last time Jacob ordered my favorite, he told me he had proposed to Alyssa, and the time before that, he told me they were moving in together.

"Pull the band-aid," I said as I picked up one of the sticks.

"She's pregnant," Jacob said with a big smile.

"What!" I said, dropping the stick back on the plate.

Jacob and I had tried for another child multiple times, and it never happened. The specialist said it was by pure luck that I had got pregnant the first time, as Jacob had a meager sperm count, and the sperm he had were low activity. She said it was a rare condition, which meant the chances of us getting pregnant again were very low.

"I know!" Jacob said as he continued to smile.

'That fucking bitch!' I thought as he stared at me. I could rip her head right off her shoulders if she were here.

"You're mad," Jacob said as he saw the look on my face.

"How?" I asked.

"I don't know," Jacob shook his head. "We weren't even trying; Alyssa had gotten used to the idea that we would never have our own kids. And last night, she told me we were expecting."

I didn't know what to say. Part of me wanted to ask if he was sure it was his, but I knew Alyssa. She wouldn't do a thing like that, not even if someone threatened her. She was more loyal than a dog.

"Say something," Jacob said; this time, he stopped smiling.

"What do you want me to say," I said, pushing the plate away. "You want me to be happy? Fine, I am happy for Clayton. He has always wanted a baby brother or sister. There I said it!"

"Wow, way to be mature," Jacob shook his head. "Remind me again who cheated on who?"

I shook my head and looked at him.

"I get it," I nodded. "I cheated. I sucked Johnny's cock. I am the reason that baby isn't inside me. I wake up to that realization every single day, but you need to stop rubbing your happiness in my face!"

Jacob nodded. "It wasn't my intention, I thought we were friends, and you would want to hear it from me, and not someone else."

"Congratulations," I said as I stood up. "Good luck with the marriage and the baby and everything else, but from now on, let me hear it from someone else, this," I said as I motioned at the table and then to the both of us, "Is too hard on me, so can you do that? Please?"

Jacob nodded. "I'm sorry."

I nodded and then walked out of the bar. I walked to my car and got in.

I couldn't believe it.

That was the final nail in the coffin of our relationship. After the divorce, I thought there was a chance. Then he got with Alyssa, and I thought she would be too straight-laced for him. Then they moved in together, and I thought I would have to be a good friend, and eventually, he would see what he was missing. Then the marriage was announced, and I started to feel like he was slipping away, and now he was going to be a father.

Jacob would never leave Alyssa now, not while she was pregnant or after the baby was born. Jacob wasn't that type of man. He wouldn't leave her for all the money in the world.

I started crying, knowing it was all my fault, all of it.

There was a knock on the passenger window, and I saw Kate standing there. I hit the unlock button, and she came inside.

"I just heard and knew he would want to tell you," Kate said as she hugged me and pulled me close.

I broke down immediately.

"It's okay," Kate said as she held me and stroked my hair. "It's okay."

IT WASN'T OKAY, NOT at all. They sped up the date of their marriage from four months to three days. They had a small wedding at a church, then a small reception at their house. It was official; they were legally married.

Clayton showed me pictures of the wedding and the reception. He didn't mean to upset me. He was just happy for his dad and now his stepmom. Clayton was over the moon about having a baby sister or brother.

The dreams of sleeping with Jacob were no more. It was like my mind had officially thrown in the towel. I was alone. Even when I was at the bar, and guys hit on me, I felt alone.

I had always heard about the pain that never disappeared after your heart broke but never experienced it until now. No matter how much I slept or drank, it lingered, never stopping, never taking a break.

I had given birth to a child and broken three bones and many other things, but nothing hurt this much, physically or mentally.

"You can't keep doing this," Kate said as she entered my house. "It's been over two months."

"Why not," I said as I poured another drink. "I am not outside, and I don't invite anyone over."

"I didn't say you were going to do something stupid," Kate said as she took the bottle from my hand. "You still have Clayton."

"No," I said, shaking my head. "I have Clayton for now," I corrected as I looked at her. "You think he will want to come over here when the baby comes?"

"Yes," Katie said. "You forget how much a baby cries, and how much attention it needs? Clayton will want to come over a lot more, just to get away."

I thought about it for a few moments. "Nope," I said, shaking my head. "Clayton loves to help; he will want to help do everything for it."

"So, you're just going to drink and drink, until what?" Katie asked. "What's the end game here?"

"There is none," I shrugged. "It dulls the pain and the thoughts," I said as I pulled the bottle away from her. "You should be pointing and laughing and saying I told you so," I said as I slumped onto the couch. "After all you were yelling at me to stop, right?"

Katie shook her head. "I will come back when you're sober," she said as she walked towards the door.

SOBRIETY DIDN'T LAST long. It only came when I went to work, and the few weekends I had Clayton. Then one day, I heard a noise outside my back door.

"Oh, it's you," I said as I saw Andrew as I looked out the back window.

"The parts came, I will get started, shouldn't take me long, a week or less," Andrew said.

"Take your time," I said as I returned to the living room.

There was a knock on my front door.

"What?" I asked, thinking it was Kate. She had been giving me the silent treatment for a couple of days.

"You look like shit," Andrew said as he stared at me.

I wore a long shirt with no bra on and white jogging pants. My hair was messy. It was Sunday, and I had nowhere to go. I hadn't showered since I left for work Friday morning, so I was sure I looked and smelt like the way I felt inside.

"Thanks, what do you want?" I asked as I went back to my chair.

He flicked a picture onto my lap. I looked at it and saw a pretty black woman standing next to him.

"She's short," I said as I looked at it.

"Taller than you," Andrew said as he took it back.

"Wife?" I asked.

"Ex," Andrew said as he put it back in his wallet.

"Sorry to hear," I said, picking up my drink.

"After I came back, I wasn't the same," Andrew said as he sat down. "None of us really come back the same as we left," he said, nodding his head, "But they always say buck up, go to the meetings and charge ahead."

I stared at him. "You served?"

"Yup," Andrew nodded. He lifted his arm sleeve and showed the tattoo he had. I had seen something like it several times around the bar and at work.

"I didn't know," I nodded.

"How were you supposed to," Andrew said.

"So, what happened?" I asked.

"I went to the meetings, did the rounds, took the medications," Andrew nodded. "But couldn't get things right, then one day I stopped. I stopped going to the meetings, stopped doing the rounds, and stopped the medication, all of it."

"Hit rock bottom," I nodded.

"The lowest," Andrew nodded. "Started finding peace and quiet in the bottom of a bottle, just like yours."

I looked at the bottle and back at him.

"One day, we got into a heated argument, and she left out the door in a hurry," Andrew said. Tears swelled up in his eyes. "They said she was doing over eighty when her car hit the tree," he nodded. "Eighty miles per hour," he shook his head. "Dead on impact."

My eyes widened.

"I vowed that day, I would never pick up another bottle ever again," Andrew said. "Whatever you're looking for, you won't find it in all the bottles in the world, I just thought you should know," he stood up and walked towards the door.

After Andrew left, I stared at the bottle, and for what seemed like over an hour, I just swirled it around and around, watching the liquid inside spin in circles. Finally, I went to the sink and poured it all out.

"Time to get back on the horse," I said as I watched the brown liquid go down the drain.

"WELCOME BACK," KATE said as I went to her house the following day.

"Sorry," I nodded.

"Nothing to be sorry about," Kate smiled. "We all fall off. Glad to see you get back on," she said. "So, what's the plan?"

"Nothing," I shrugged. "No plan, going to take it one day at a time."

"Sounds good to me," Kate smiled.

We talked for a while, and then I headed out. I had taken the day off and wanted to do some me time.

I drove around for a while and found myself outside Alyssa's workplace.

I walked inside, and Alyssa's eyes widened as she saw me. She was sitting behind the reception desk, taking information from one of the patients.

When the patient left, I stepped up to the desk.

"First," I said as I cleared my throat, "I want to say I am sorry for how I have treated you these past years," I nodded. "You're good to my son and good to Jacob, and I have trashed talked you and belittled you as often as I could, and I am sorry."

Alyssa nodded and stared at me.

"Second, congratulations, even though we have different ideals and ways of raising a child, I think you will be a great mother," I nodded.

"That means a lot to me," Alyssa nodded.

"Third and final," I said as I leaned in close. "Hurt either of them, in any shape or form, they will never, and I mean never, find your body," I said, staring at Alyssa's blue eyes. "Do I make myself clear?"

Alyssa smiled. "You can leave now," she said as she looked at the patients behind me.

I nodded and slowly walked out the door.

"The bitch is back," I said as I looked back and saw Alyssa talking on her phone.

No doubt talking to Jacob.

A few minutes later, my phone rang. It was Jacob. I didn't answer it. There was no need to hear what he had to say. I said what I said, and I meant it.

"What the fuck do you want?" Hank asked as he opened the door of his hotel.

"You ever, and I mean ever come around my house again," I said as I aimed my gun at his crotch.

Hank's eyes were wide open, and I pushed my way inside. I slammed the door behind me.

"Sorry!" Hank said as he looked around, no doubt for his gun or something to hit me with. I pushed it into him harder.

"You are going to leave me alone, Jacob alone, and definitely Clayton alone," I said as I stared at him.

Hank nodded.

"Good," I said as I put it away.

I waited for him to say something, anything.

"That it?" Hank asked as he calmed down.

"No, but it's the start," I smiled.

"Glad to see the old you return," Hank said as he lit a cigarette." It seems like my job here is done."

I shook my head. "Thanks."

"No problem, we all need a kick in the ass," Hank said as he handed me a cigarette.

I hadn't smoked since I knew I was pregnant with Clayton.

I looked at it reluctantly and then shrugged. The first drag made me cough, but I got used to it afterward.

"o, now what?" Hank asked. "She back for good, or just until she feels like being all goody two shoes again?"

"No idea," I shrugged. "I can't be like I was, that's for sure."

"What? No orgies and group sex, just for the fuck of it?" Hank asked.

"Nope," I shook my head. "But I am tired of playing the victim, tired of apologizing and playing the good person all the time."

"Amen to that," Hank nodded. "So, something in the middle, not like your parents, but not like the married wife, something in between?"

"Exactly," I nodded. "What are you going to do?"

"Head out tomorrow," Hank nodded. "I heard about you being all bent out of shape and now you're all straightened out," Hank shrugged. "Time for me to go."

"You know you didn't do this right?" I shook my head.

"No, but if I wasn't here, you wouldn't have gotten pissed, and you would have tried to find some way of apologizing again," Hank smiled.

I nodded that part was true, he did start me on the road, so I had to give him that much.

"One last ride before I go," Hank smiled, looking at the bed.

"Not if you were the last man on earth," I said, standing up. "Have a good one Hank."

"You too Shelly," Hank said.

I drove home and saw Jacob's truck parked in my driveway.

I smiled as I saw him standing outside talking to Andrew. I pulled in and got out of the car.

"What the fuck is your problem?" Jacob yelled at me.

"You tell me," I shouted back. "What did you expect?"

"Oh, you're smoking again?" Jacob asked as he came close to me, no doubt smelling the cigarette I had at Hanks.

"Maybe," I yelled back. "Again, none of your business."

"Well, threatening my wife is," Jacob said.

"Not a threat, a promise, something I should have done years ago," I said as I walked past him.

"I am not done yet," Jacob yelled.

"Well, I am," I yelled back. "Now kindly, get the fuck off my property."

Jacob looked at me, and for the first time since the divorce, I think he finally saw the old me, not the woman he had married and changed. I was the bitch that took his virginity in the woods.

The one that pushed him down to the ground yanked his pants down and rode his long white cock on the dirt ground until he came inside her, not once or twice, but three times. That was the woman he was looking at now.

"What?" I asked. "You forgot how to drive? Get in the driver's seat push the button that starts the engine and drive that piece of shit Ford off my property."

Jacob slowly walked back to his truck. He stared at me as I stood in my doorway. I stared back at him.

I watched as he pulled away.

"Nice," Andrew nodded.

"You approve?" I asked.

"Definitely," Andrew nodded. "He's had it coming for a long time now."

"I am sure I will hear about it later," I nodded.

"Then deal with it later," Andrew smiled.

I nodded again. "You need help?" I asked. "I feel like hitting something with a hammer," I said.

"How about using a power tool?" Andrew asked as he pointed to the giant saw.

"Yes!" I yelled as I walked towards his truck.

Chapter Six: Acceptance of Change

Not many people liked the new me, which I knew would happen. The changes were difficult for some people to process. Especially for those who didn't know me before I married Jacob. Those that did loved it.

"Up here," I smiled as I looked at the guy before me. "They won't get your drinks, I will."

"Sorry, but they are just so big," the man smiled.

"I know. I carry them around all day," I nodded. "What do you want?"

The new me no longer wore clothes that tried to hide my large chest, or did I try to hide anything about my body, my wide hips, or my big ass. I wore tight jeans and tight, low-cut shirts.

Of course, I always got significant comments that I shouldn't wear that, or I only have big boobs because I was a big woman, but it didn't stop them from staring or even asking for my number.

I left the warehousing job and went full-time at the bar, which was paying off, as since I was there every night, my tips were through the roof.

I flicked my fingers again in the face of the same guy and smiled. "You really have to order," I said.

"Right," he said as he shook his head.

It was like this most nights, especially on the weekends. I made a killing on tips during the sports games. I had invested in some of the local team's shirts and cut a deep V into them so my chest would stick out. It was a massive hit with both men and women.

The most significant turnaround for me was Jacob and Alyssa. A week after our argument, they arrived at my house without Clayton.

They both apologized for treating me like I was a bad person. Jacob admitted that while I had cheated on him, it didn't give him the right to throw it in my face every chance he got, especially after I apologized and gave him a speedy divorce without fighting him.

I promised to stay out of their way and not talk badly about their relationship. It was the least I could do. So far, I held my end of the bargain, and so did they; Clayton was getting excited about having a new kid to play with, and I had to tell him it would be a long while before the baby would be able to play with him, and by then he would be a teenager and might not want to play with it.

It didn't change his mind any.

"So," the young man said as I finally gave him his drink.

"So," I said as I looked at him.

He was a young man who was probably in his early twenties and was very good-looking. With a muscular body, which I guessed he loved to show off due to his tight muscle shirt.

"When do you get out?" he asked.

"Me or them?" I asked.

"I deserved that," he nodded.

"Yes, you did," I smiled. "The three of us get out at two, that might be past your bedtime."

"Deserved that, also," he nodded. "Jason," he said, introducing himself.

"Shelly, or Shells," I said as we shook hands.

I went around the bar, ensuring everyone's drinks were filled and no one felt left out, but I returned to Jason occasionally.

"So, what do you have in mind?" I asked as I started closing just before two in the morning.

"Well," Jason said as he stared right at my tits.

"You know there is more to my body than just tits, right?" I flirted back at him.

"Yeah," Jason smiled. "I definitely noticed."

Jason's hands were all over me as soon as we left the bar. As usual, he was all hands and no brain. I had stuck to my original plan, no sex, just fun.

And while Jason thought this night would end with his cock inside me, I made sure I brought him back down to earth as quickly as possible.

"No," I said as he tried to pull me towards his truck.

"Follow me," I said as I got in my car.

We went to a local area near the lake, and I climbed out and got into the back of his truck. Again, he was too excited for anything lasting to happen. By the time I got his cock out and into my mouth, I could feel he was on the verge of cumming.

All it took was a few bobs of my head on his cock, and he held my head down as he came.

"That's disappointing," I said as I wiped my mouth.

"It's okay," Jason smiled. "I got a few more in me, you know what they say about young guys," he said with a toothy grin.

"Well, let's see what you got," I said as I unbuckled my belt.

Two minutes he lasted as he tried to go down on me. Even with me giving him hints of what to do, he fumbled around and then gave up.

"Nope," I said as he tried to push himself onto me. "If I don't get off, neither do you."

"Fucking tease!" Jason yelled as I pulled my pants up.

"That goes for the both of us," I said as I jumped down from his truck.

"Fucking Slut!" Jason yelled at me as he slammed his door.

"You would have had to fuck me, to call me that, you fucking moron!" I yelled back.

Jason's truck skidded off as he gave me the middle finger.

It wasn't the first time one of them got all in their feelings about me not letting them fuck me, but I was in it for fun and the thrill, not the sex.

"ONE NIGHT, ONE OF THEM are going to try and do something more," Rachel said. The following night.

She was the other bartender that worked with me. "And that's what your there for," I smiled.

Rachel was a crack shot; we went to the range several times, and I always thought Hank and Jacob were the best with guns. No, this little five-foot-two blonde was terrific with all firearms, big or small. She outdid all the guys there.

"One night, I won't," Rachel said.

"And on that night, I won't go," I smiled.

Rachel shook her head.

It was a two-way street for us. Rachel always got the guys that weren't interested in the big girls, and I got the guys that didn't like the small girls. We were a great tag team. We always went to the same place. Either I hid in my car a few feet away, or she hid in hers to ensure no one tried anything.

After a few weeks, the fun at the bar started to end as Rachel found a nice guy named Ryan, and he was a city cowboy, as some would call him. He loved country music and wearing cowboy boots and hats but lived downtown. He had never lived out in the sticks, unlike Rachel, who had grown up in a place I had never heard about until she mentioned it.

Ryan was good to her from the start. He didn't go with her to the lake; instead, he gave her his number and called it a night. Ryan showed up every Saturday night, drank the same thing, and ordered the same cheeseburger with fries.

"One day, you will find one," Rachel said as she looked at Ryan.

"Nope," I said, shaking my head.

I was beginning to think I wasn't the relationship type.

I got off work, but I turned down any pursuers this time as I had somewhere to be in the morning. Clayton was home, and I wanted to get in immediately.

"WAKE UP!" CLAYTON YELLED as he pushed me back and forth.

"I am up," I said as I looked at him.

I looked at the time, "Clayton, bud, you got two hours," I said, turning over.

"Yeah, but you take long to get ready," Clayton said.

"It's a monster truck rally," I said as I looked at him as he had run around to the other side of the bed. "I can go like this and fit right on in."

"You're not going to do that are you?" Clayton asked.

"It's a joke," I said as I sat up.

I knew he wouldn't let it go until I was ready. "Okay, go start the coffee and I will be right down," I said.

"Thanks," he said as he took off.

Andrew had gotten us tickets to the sold-out monster truck show downtown. I didn't know how he got them, but he was picking us up from my house in a few to take us down there.

Katie was through the roof that he was taking Darold with us. She liked the idea that Darold spent time with a black male. All the guys that had shown her any interest always frowned when she mentioned she had a half-black son.

"Maybe he has a brother," Kate said as she dropped off Darold.

"Take him," I said as I watched the three guys playing football in my front yard. Andrew was throwing it, and the two were running around catching it.

"I think he is interested in you," Katie smiled.

"No," I shook my head. "We are friends, that's it."

"Uh-huh," Katie nodded.

Andrew and I finished the deck weeks ago, and then he showed me how to install ceiling fans so I could change the rest by myself. He called me now and then to help him with other side projects, and we have been close friends ever since.

I told him about my past and what happened with Jacob, and he laughed. No one had laughed before. They always looked at me with that judgmental look, but he laughed and shook his head, and that was it.

Andrew told me about his past marriage and how it lasted between them, even with him going overseas and on many tours, but it ended badly.

"Did you see...." Clayton said as we got out of the show.

"Yes, Clayton I was sitting right beside you," I said, shaking my head.

I loved seeing Clayton and Darold like this; they talked nonstop. Before they would finish a sentence, another was hot on its tail.

Andrew opened the door for me and walked around the truck. I got inside and opened his door. The boys got in the back, and we headed back home.

"Want to stop and get dinner?" I asked.

"Sure," Andrew nodded.

Andrew lived in a double-wide trailer a few miles outside of my town. I had only seen the outside as he never allowed me to enter.

I guessed it was a total mess inside there. Andrew didn't disagree or agree with me.

"Fuck no!" I said as I looked at his shopping cart.

"What?" Andrew asked.

We had gone to the grocery store as I wanted to make dinner for the boys and me. Andrew was picking things up for himself.

"Just no," I said, shaking my head.

Andrew's shopping cart was filled with single-guy food, many canned types of meat, some microwaveable plastic cup things, and a shit ton of microwaveable frozen foods.

"Put all that shit back," I said, shaking my head.

"What?" Andrew smiled.

"No, put all of it right back where you got it," I said without a smile on my face.

"You know, you can be a pain, right?" Andrew asked.

"Yup, a pain that won't allow anyone to buy that shit," I said. "What the fuck is this?"

"Chipped beef," Andrew said as I held up a bottle of what looked like red cardboard inside.

"Fuck no," I said as I took him around the store. "You see this section, it's called Produce, it's where we get fresh vegetables and fruit."

"I know," Andrew said. "I had fruit in my cart."

"Fruit in plastic cups swimming in sugar water, is not considered fruit, now get some real fruit." I said. "No!"

I slapped the box of fake banana bread out of his hand. "Bad!" I yelled. A couple passing us smiled, and she pointed to her man and nodded at me.

"What took you guys so long?" the boys asked as we returned to the truck.

"I had to teach this one how to grocery shop," I said, pulling the seatbelt over me. "He's coming for dinner so I can show him how to cook also."

"I can cook," Andrew said.

"Using the microwave isn't cooking!" I shook my head.

I WAVED AS ANDREW'S truck pulled out of the driveway later that night.

"You like him," Kate said as I returned to the house.

Darold and Clayton were fast asleep on the couch, and we didn't have it in us to wake them.

Kate would take the guest room as usual and take Darold home in the morning.

"Why do you say that?" I asked.

"You cooked for him," Katie said.

"I am a big girl I love to cook," I shrugged as we cleaned up the table.

"You gave him leftovers," Kate smiled. "Don't say you give leftovers to everybody because you only do it for Jacob."

Jacob still loved my cooking. Especially my Italian dishes.

"You should have seen his shopping cart," I said, shaking my head. "It was the poster for single man dinners, there must have been at least fourteen of those frozen food dinners."

Kate shook her head. "He might as well fill a plate with salt and eat it with a spoon."

"Exactly," I said.

"So, am I right?" Kate asked as we put dishes in the washer.

"I don't know, to be honest," I nodded. "I want to, if that makes sense, but he is very quiet about his past, and that's just a huge red flag for me."

"Most military guys don't talk about what happened to them. It's easier for them to cope with it, if they don't say it out loud," Katie nodded.

I nodded, but there was something more to it than that. Andrew had a lot of scars on his arms and chest. And it was bothering me.

"You could ask Lyle, he might know," Katie said.

"Good idea," I nodded.

We made sure everything was locked up and rechecked on the boys. I knew they would wake up sometime during the night and go upstairs to their beds.

I had bought two beds for Clayton's room, knowing Darold would spend many nights over here. Kate had done the same thing for Darold's room.

"Oh," Katie said as we started to head up to bed. "He might not have a fourteen-inch dick, just throwing that out there."

I shook my head.

"Also, all of them don't want to shove their cock up your ass," she smiled.

"I wouldn't mind if he wanted to," I shrugged.

"Whore!" Katie smiled.

"That's queen whore," I smiled back at her.

THE NEXT DAY AFTER I dropped Clayton off to Jacob, I headed to the VA bar across town.

"Woah!" Lyle said as I opened the door.

"I know, not a member," I nodded. "And after what my dad did here, I knew it would be better to come now, before it got busy."

My dad was a lousy drunk, and one night, he came in here spitting words like fake valor and many things that were not good to say around a bunch of military people.

Dad always thought the military was for people that couldn't hack it in the real world. But he consistently voted Republican every voting day, rain, sleet, or shine.

"Good idea," Lyle said as he looked at the few people in the corner. "What brings you here?"

"Do you know Andrew? I don't know his last name," I said, sitting at the bar.

"You're going to have to be more specific," Lyle nodded.

"Really tall, black guy, arm tattoos. He looks like he can wrestle a bear and win," I said.

"Duke!" Lyle nodded.

"Duke?" I asked.

"His parents are from England, we always call him Duke or some British title," Lyle smiled. "Yeah, he comes in once in a while, just to hang out, doesn't drink, because of," Lyle stopped. "Shelly? You aren't doing what I think you are?"

Before Lyle went to the military, he had heard about my actions in the locker room, and when he returned, he got the full scope of everything I had done while he was gone.

"No, those days are long gone," I nodded.

"Good, Andrew's been through enough," Lyle said as he came around the bar to sit near me.

"I was hoping you would shed some light on that," I whispered as he sat near me.

"His last tour he and his squad got ambushed, things went sideways fast," Lyle whispered. "Can't give you the details, but needless to say he was the only survivor," Lyle said as he looked at the others.

"Fuck," I said.

Lyle motioned for me to be quiet. "That's not all, he completed the task himself, even after all of that," Lyle said. "The guys around here always stand when he comes in, not one of them stay seated. For someone to complete what he did, by himself, after seeing your squad torn to shreds, that's some deep mental shit."

I nodded. "I didn't hear a thing," I said as I stood up.

"Shelly, if you're being real this time, get him back on his meds, he might not think he needs them, but he does," Lyle said.

I nodded again.

I quickly drove across town and showed up at the Drayson's house. I saw Andrew working on their garage door.

"Hi," I said.

"Hi," Andrew nodded.

I stood still and looked at him.

"I didn't go back to the store," Andrew said as he looked back at me.

"What's going on?" I asked.

I knew Andrew liked being direct, so I was straightforward with him.

"With what exactly?" Andrew said as he turned to face me.

"This," I said as I stared up at him. "Us?"

"I don't know," Andrew shrugged. "Was leaving that up to you."

Andrew picked up another tool and started working on the door again.

"If it's what I think it is, then I need to know things," I said.

Andrew nodded as he put the tool down. "Okay, like what?" he asked.

I grabbed his long sleeve, pulled it up, and looked at the long scar that started at the wrist and went up to his bicep. I pulled on the other arm, and he stopped me.

"Shelly, there are some things best left unsaid," Andrew said as he held my hand.

"Not to me," I said as I stared at him.

I tiptoed and kissed him. "I am not leaving," I said as I looked at him.

"Fine," Andrew said. "You really want to know?"

"Like I said, not going anywhere," I said, folding my arms.

Andrew told me everything about what they were doing there, what the intel had told them, and that it was supposed to be a walk in the park, get some hostages, and return home.

Everything was wrong, they were ambushed from all sides, and the night turned into day with ammunition fire. They had nowhere to hide and were pinned down.

I didn't bat an eye even though inside, I was bawling. He told me that after the firing stopped, the enemy combatants walked through the bodies of his squad to ensure everyone was dead.

Andrew pulled what was left of his friend over him and lay still. They passed over him. He said he still saw their faces when he went to bed.

Then he got up and went one by one, slowly knocking them off. Rescued the hostages and returned.

His face told it all. As he talked about it, it was like he was back there, his hands trembled, and his face shook.

"Andrew," I said as I held his head. "I'm still here," I smiled. "See, not going anywhere."

He hugged me, and I took his hand. "I will come back and finish up," I nodded at the two old couple standing inside the garage. I am sure they heard everything.

"What are we doing?" Andrew asked as I pulled up to the VA bar.

"Getting you help," I nodded as Lyle and a few others exited the bar.

"We got it from here," Lyle nodded. Lyle and a few others walked Andrew back inside.

JACOB'S TRUCK CAME skidding to a stop as I was back at the Drayson's house.

Jacob climbed down and came over. "You have no clue what you are doing, do you?" he asked as he saw me looking at the garage door.

"Not a fricking clue," I smiled.

"I'll help," he said, removing his button shirt and throwing it to the ground.

We got to work on the door together.

"You made me proud today," Jacob said as he worked on the door.

"Wasn't my intention," I said, handing him another tool. "It was the right thing to do."

"He's going to be okay, thanks to you," Jacob said as he looked at me.

"Hope so," I smiled.

We both laughed for a bit. "Who knew the whore of Windsor High School had a soft spot?" Jacob laughed.

"Hey! All of that happened after I graduated," I said, smacking him.

"Uh-huh," Jacob smiled. "Keep telling yourself that," he laughed.

Chapter Seven: New and Improved

Things were getting better for me, at least on the forefront. The relationship between Andrew and I was starting to blossom. He admitted himself to the local hospital a few days ago as he began thinking thoughts that he knew were bad for himself and wanted to get some help.

I knew it was good for him, and it was the right thing to do, especially if it meant keeping him around. There were no visitation hours as they wanted him to sort himself out and get him on the proper medication.

Conversely, it gave me time to sort other things out, namely his trailer.

I got some of the guys from the VA bar to help me break into his trailer. It shocked all of us.

It was a hoarder's dream, they offered to help me get it back in order, but I took it upon myself to clean it all up.

Kate also came over to help voluntarily. I bet she wished she didn't now.

The first day I spent trying to find the horrid smell that was making me gag. The next day I found it later in the day. It was the refrigerator. Immediately Katie and I got that unplugged, tapped the doors closed with duct table, and got it outside, which was a task in itself.

Jacob and Jesse got us a sizeable open-top dumpster and helped us get most of the big things into it.

"I can't believe you two got it out here yourself," Jesse said as we got the large refrigerator into the dumpster.

I still didn't like him, but he was offering to help, so I put up with his presence for now.

"Girl power," Kate smiled as she flexed her muscles.

"Is he okay with you cleaning this out?" Jacob asked.

"Yes and no," I nodded as we went back inside.

"You haven't told him," Jacob nodded.

"Yes and no," I smiled.

"She told him that she had a surprise for him when he got out," Kate said.

"Exactly," I nodded.

"He might not like you digging into his privacy," Jesse said.

"Hypocrite," I replied.

Jesse nodded as I looked at him.

"I heard through the grapevine you're dating again," Jesse said, quickly changing the subject.

"Yes," Kate nodded as we put the trash into the big black bags.

The place was a dumpster filled with old magazines, fast food trash, and soda cans. We could hardly see the ground underneath all of it.

"Anyone we know?" Jacob asked.

"Nope, and I will leave it at that," Kate smiled.

I knew all about it, his name was Timothy, and she had met him online on one of her dating apps; so far, they had gone on five dates, and she liked him.

I could tell by Jesse's face that he wasn't happy. He had a thing for Kate and had tried multiple times to get her to notice him, but she had no interest in him, mainly because he had the same reaction as I when she told us about Darold's father.

While I said what I thought to her face, Jesse had told his thoughts to a couple of people, and it got around, so needless to say, his chances of Kate ever paying any attention to him were nonexistent.

Throw in the fact he wasn't her type, and those odds went further downhill.

Katie was an attractive woman. Well, put together, as some would say when they looked at her. There was no glaring thing that made her gorgeous. She had average C cups, an average body build, and long mouse-brown hair.

The day slowly ended, and we could finally see the linoleum flooring in the living room. The kitchen and the rest of the other rooms would have to wait for another day. We also threw out the couch. It also reeked and had stains all over it.

"YOU AGAIN," I SAID as I shook my head.

I was working the late shift at the bar, and Jason sat down as I was preparing another person's drink.

"It's a free world, right?" Jason asked.

"Sure." I shrugged. "What can I get you?"

Jason ordered a drink and immediately started trying to impress me to go on another date. I laughed at his many attempts to prove that he wasn't as selfish as he had come across that night.

I always loved it when a guy said he could prove he wasn't selfish by asking any of his exes. Who says that and means it?

"Look," I said as I stared at him. "And I mean this in the nicest way possible, I am starting to see someone, and I think it will get serious, so, I have to say I am not interested," I said as I tried to let him down gently.

"Fine, whatever," Jason said as he stood up. "Just wanted to get laid anyway."

"Absolutely," I nodded. "Totally understandable."

"Okay," Jason said as he paid for his drinks and walked away.

Rachel and I had a good laugh after he left.

"Look what the cat dragged in," I smiled as I saw Lyle walking towards the bar.

He ordered a drink, and I poured it out for him.

"What brings you this way?" I asked.

"Just wanted to see how the other side lived," Lyle smiled.

Lyle and I had a history in high school, not the sexual kind, but he wanted more than I was willing to give. Then after high school, he joined the military, and I became the neighborhood slut.

When Lyle returned home, he heard about my escapades and found out I was married to Jacob, an old friend of his, and had a child. We didn't talk much after that. Now here he sat in my bar.

"What do you think?" I asked.

"Not as nice as mine, but it's okay," Lyle smiled.

"Thanks, we try," I nodded.

"I heard you are cleaning up Andrew's place," Lyle said with a serious look on his face.

"Yeah, thought it would be nice for him to come home to a clean place, might help him recover," I said.

"I have to ask," Lyle said.

"Don't," I said, shaking my head.

"I have heard you have done things like this before, and..." Lyle said.

"Look," I said as I stared him right in the eyes. "I fucked up, I am a big girl I can admit it, I drank too much and got carried away, the end."

"What about now?" Lyle asked. "Could this be some attempt to win Jacob back, everyone knows how much you love him and his, let's say appendage."

I smiled and shook my head. "That's what people think?" I said. "I am trying to make Jacob jealous by dating a black guy?"

"Never said race," Lyle said, shaking his head.

"But that's the going theory, right?" I asked.

Lyle didn't respond.

"I like Andrew; he's blunt, he likes guns, he doesn't have a beard, and he accepts me as a person. All of me, the past, the present, and the future."

"The past?" Lyle asked.

"All of it, he knows, everything," I nodded. "Unlike some people he knows that people can change."

"Okay," Lyle said as he lifted his hands and waved one of the white napkins. "I had to know for sure, he is one of us, and I wanted to make sure he was in good hands, that's all."

I nodded. "Now, how about you?"

Lyle looked at me as I shook my head. "You still haven't apologized for giving me the cold shoulder for how many years now?"

Lyle smiled. "You're right," he paused and looked at me, "For me, you are the one that got away," he said as he stared into my eyes. "I had a huge crush on you, and you made me feel like I was in the wrong for feeling that way. I went away thinking you would see me differently when I returned, and that didn't happen," he shrugged.

Lyle swirled his cup and stared at it. Then looked up at me. "That wasn't your fault, it was mine and I need to get over that, someday."

"I wasn't ready for a relationship. Hell, I didn't want one, not even with Jacob," I smiled. "I liked having fun and doing what I wanted to do, when I wanted to do it, and with who I wanted. no commitments. You wanted a girlfriend. That wasn't me. After we graduated, I did everything I wanted to do and more."

I had many thoughts during high school but never acted on them because I knew my parents would literally kill me and whoever I did it with, but after the moment passed, I let it all out.

"What happened with Jacob was a one in a million, and it paid off. We had a great marriage, have a wonderful son, and now we are good friends."

It even shocked me to say that, but these past few weeks with Andrew had made me see that Jacob had moved on, and it was time for me to do the same.

"Andrew is a lucky man," Lyle said.

"We are both lucky," I nodded.

"Well, I better get back to my side of the tracks," Lyle said as he opened his wallet.

"On the house," I nodded.

"Thanks," Lyle said. "If there is anything me or the guys can do for you to get Andrew's place ready, let us know."

"Actually," I smiled.

IT TOOK A FEW MORE days to get the place looking good. Jacob came through with a professional cleaning crew to clean everything after most of the trash was taken to the dumpster. I had to admit it was a nice trailer after it got cleaned up.

Lyle and some of the guys worked their magic and got Andrew all new kitchen appliances, a new couch, and a bed. I didn't know how they managed to get everything in there, but it made the place more livable.

All we had to do was wait for the main guy.

Andrew was due to come out tomorrow, and I had butterflies in my stomach and was excited to see him again.

"Looks good," Jacob said as he joined me in one more walk-through, I liked having him around these past few days.

"Looks a lot better," I nodded.

"You did good," Jacob smiled.

"We did good," I said as I shook his hand.

No other ex-husband would help their ex-wife clean up her new boyfriend's place. Jacob was one of a kind.

"Sorry again for putting you through all that crap," Jacob said.

"We both need to stop apologizing to each other," I nodded.

"Deal," Jacob said, shaking my hand again.

I went back home and went to sleep.

SOME OF THE GUYS FROM the bar went to pick Andrew up from the hospital. We all waited inside the bar. Everyone was there. Kate and her new boyfriend, as well as Jacob and Alyssa. Clayton was excited to see his friend.

I was not too fond of waiting around. I kept looking back at the door and wishing it to open and Andrew to walk in. The moment arrived, and the place exploded with hand claps and cheers.

Everyone was thankful he was back among us. I smiled as Andrew went around, thanking everyone and smiling. When he got close to me, he shook his head.

"Thank you," Andrew said. "Not many people stand up to me, the way you did."

"Well, that's because most people have a clear head on their shoulders," I smiled.

"No, most people stick to themselves and do not care about anyone else," Andrew said. "You have a good heart, and it's a good trait to have," Andrew said as he hugged me tightly.

"Just a hug?" I asked.

"Nope," Andrew smiled with that big giant smile as he kissed me.

Again, the place clapped and cheered.

We celebrated Andrew's return, and he told me the regimen they would put him on; he had to have visits and a therapist as well as medication, and I told him I would keep him to everything this time.

Afterward, some of us returned to the trailer. Andrew was nervous about stepping inside. He could already tell that we cleaned the outside.

I watched as he took it all in.

"I cleaned the windows," Clayton said.

"I helped," Darold added.

"It's great," Andrew nodded as he pulled Clayton next to him and patted him on the shoulders. "I feel embarrassed that you guys had to see it the way it was," he said, shaking his head.

"That's the past," I said, holding his hand.

Andrew nodded.

Everyone stuck around for a few minutes before they all left. Kate took Clayton back to her place, and I waited in the kitchen as Andrew said goodbye to some of his friends.

"You angry?" I asked as he came back inside.

"Not at all," Andrew said.

"I threw away a lot of stuff," I admitted.

Andrew hugged and gripped me tightly. His hands gripped my ass as he held me close to him.

"I am not angry at all," he grinned.

"Good, because the place smelled," I smiled as I tip-toed to kiss him.

"Sorry you had to go through all of that," Andrew said with both his hands firmly on my ass.

"Well, there is something you can do to make it up to me," I grinned.

Andrew lifted me onto the kitchen counter with a tight grip and a quick jerk. For a big girl like me, that was a feat no other guy had done.

"What is it?" Andrew asked as he looked at me.

"Well, you can start by kissing me again," I said.

"Done," Andrew said as we kissed again. He held me so tight this time I thought my seams would burst.

When he let me go, he stared down at my chest. I had worn a low-cut shirt that showed a lot of my cleavage.

"Want to see?" I asked. I already knew the answer by the look on his face.

I grabbed the bottom of my shirt and slowly pulled it over my head. I smiled as he stared speechless at my L-cup breasts trapped in my bra.

"They usually have that effect on guys," I smiled as I pulled him close to me and between my legs using his belt. "Your turn."

I watched as he unbuckled his belt and dropped his pants. While I wasn't expecting fourteen or twelve inches, what I saw still impressed me. It wasn't as long as Jacobs, but it was definitely thicker.

"My," I said, staring at it as it throbbed up and down.

"Good enough for the size queen?" Andrew asked.

"Definitely, yes," I nodded.

I scootched forward and pulled my jeans off, then my underwear. I was about to get down, but Andrew lifted me off the counter.

"Holy fuck!" I yelled as Andrew impaled me onto his cock.

My legs instantly wrapped around him, and my arms around his neck.

"Better?" Andrew asked as he slowly started to bounce me onto his cock.

I had never been fucked standing up before, many had tried, but they always fell back down or immediately put me down. I was a heavy woman.

"Mhmm," was all I could say as Andrew's cock pushed deeper inside me.

Andrew started slow, his arm and hands underneath me as he lifted and dropped me onto his dick.

I found new pleasure in this position, something I thought would never happen as I thought I had done it all. Andrew's cock stretched me with its thickness, and gravity did its job as it pulled me down onto his cock.

It started slowly, but Andrew gradually increased the speed as he bounced me. His hands gripped my ass as he lifted, dropped, lifted, dropped.

I was a human rag doll to him. I was getting fucked by him while standing in the middle of his kitchen. My legs involuntarily stopped wrapping around him and flopped up and down on their own.

"Fuck! Yes!" Andrew yelled and groaned as he used me as a life-sized fuck doll.

I never had in all my years felt like I was being used as I did right now. Not ever. A big girl like me was meant to be bent over and fucked or on my back and fucked, never to be wrapped around a man's waist and fucked like a cock sleeve.

Andrew's grip moved from my ass to my waist as he adjusted repeatedly. Andrew bounced me hard. I held on for my life with my arms around his neck and my head on his shoulder.

I was cumming, and it felt like nothing I had felt all my years. I had a few leg-shaking orgasms with Jacob, but none felt like what was happening to me now.

I didn't just cum. I orgasmed hard and squirted for the first time in my life. I heard the liquid splash onto the floor. It was the first time it had ever happened to me.

Andrew didn't stop. It was like he expected it to happen. If anything, it made him bounce me harder.

"Stop," I said as I could no longer feel my legs or any of my extremities.

Andrew didn't stop. Instead, he walked while carrying me across the kitchen, through the living room, and planted me on his bed with a thud.

"Fuck!" I said as Andrew put both of my legs onto his shoulders.

I knew I would get it hard in this position. My legs were high on Andrew's shoulders, and my back was against his bed.

Andrew fucked me hard, harder than before. I heard him growling and grunting as he fucked into me. His cock pounded inside me. I felt all his body weight on top of me.

My body was his to take. I thought he would never stop until I felt it, and then I felt it again. His dick was throbbing. He was about to cum.

I held him tight, with both arms wrapped around him as he came inside me.

With a loud sigh, he rolled off me onto the side of the bed beside me.

"How long has that been pent up?" I asked.

The blood slowly rushed back into my legs and toes.

"Too long," Andrew said.

I smiled as I lay down next to him.

"Hope that wasn't it for the night," I smiled.

Andrew turned over to look at me. "Not even close," he said.

WE DIDN'T GO ALL NIGHT like some fairy tale erotic story people read online. There were two more times, which left us both breathing heavily and dripping with sweat.

I left early in the morning and headed home. We planned a big day, and I wanted to get a head start.

We were spending the day out with Katie and Timothy, with the boys. First, we were going to the lake. Timothy's brother had a boat that he let Timothy borrow, so we were taking it out.

"Hey," I said as we all met at the lake.

Today was the first time I got to spend time with Timothy up close, and he was typical of Kate's type, nerdy looking with glasses, blonde hair, and blue eyes. He wasn't thin but wasn't muscular. Kate loved the nerdy types.

Andrew looked like a giant next to Timothy. Andrew stood just over seven feet tall, and I was taller than Timothy, so I guessed he was five-six, maybe seven. The boys loved the boat and wanted to see how it got in the water.

Timothy showed them how as he backed it into the water, their eyes went wide as it floated, and the hitch came back from underneath it.

Timothy was a big hit with the kids as he mastered the boat across the lake, not too fast and not too slow he kept a good pace, making sure everyone enjoyed the ride. He knew of a good place where there wasn't a lot of boat traffic.

I looked over at Kate and nodded. We were sitting in the back of the boat as all the guys were taking turns driving the boat.

"Told you," Kate said.

I nodded. Kate had told me that Timothy had taken a liking to Darold immediately. Not many of the guys she had dated before even wanted to be near Kate after she said she had a kid, let alone a mixed race one.

Timothy treated both kids equally, ensuring both got the same amount of time steering the boat.

Then the fun began as we found the spot. It was a lovely cove around a bend. There were a few others, but no one was speeding around blind corners or causing a lot of waves. So, it was perfect to go swimming.

One of the other people there let us burrow their rubber raft, and we took turns lying on it as we got pulled around.

The boys were starving and going to die soon if they didn't get something to eat, as they put it.

Luckily there was a restaurant right on the lake. We ordered and sat down. I stifled a laugh as Timothy's face went a bright red as two older women shook their heads at Darold as he walked by, and another jumped out of the way as he walked close to them.

As we finished lunch, I saw him walking toward them.

"Timothy," I said, and I shook my head.

Timothy slowly walked back to me as the others piled into Andrew's truck.

"I will go with Timothy, to drop off the boat," I said. "We will meet you at the movies."

Kate gave me a look but then nodded.

We got into his large SUV and started to drive off.

"What were you going to say, I am just curious?" I said, looking over at him.

"I was going to enlighten them on how things are done," Timothy said as he looked at me. "I was going to do it politely," he smiled.

"Uh huh," I nodded.

"What?" he asked.

"You do realize he is going to be eleven, then twelve, and so on, right?" I asked.

"Yeah," Timothy nodded.

"A teen, then a young male, then a black man," I said. "Don't let the slight difference in color fool you. A lot of people only see the black part, and none of the white."

Timothy's grip tightened on the wheel as his white knuckles turned bright red. "I know, and I am not stupid," he said, looking over at me.

"Good, because there are going to be a ton more of those moments, a shit ton," I said. "And you're not going to be there for all of them."

Timothy sighed and shook his head. "He's a good kid, he's smart, way smarter than I was at his age," Timothy smiled.

"He sure loves his books," I nodded.

"Yeah, he is reading some of mine," Timothy laughed. "Has trouble with some of the words, but he quickly grabs a dictionary and...."

I was laughing. "You know this already," Timothy nodded.

"Oh yeah," I nodded, "Why do you think I have three dictionaries in my house?" I smiled. "Clayton is going to be a jock. Darold is going to be a book nerd," I nodded.

We all knew eventually that their friendship would go two different ways. Hopefully, it would last through the differences, but only time would tell.

I LOOKED IN THE BACK seat as Andrew drove us home. "He's a good man," Andrew said.

"Yeah," I nodded.

Clayton was fast asleep in the back. After the movies and dinner, both kids fell asleep. Darold was heading home with Timothy and Kate, and Clayton was coming home with me.

Timothy was perfect for Katie; he was exactly what she was looking for and needed. I had doubts before meeting him, but after the talk, I knew he was ready for the long haul.

Andrew carried Clayton up the stairs and into his bed.

"See you in the morning?" I asked.

"Yeah," Andrew nodded.

I watched him drive off then I closed and locked the door. I went to bed and waited for the good night text from Andrew. I smiled as he told me he was home and heading for bed.

I fell asleep soon afterward.

Chapter Eight: The Right Fit

I pushed my ass backward hard as I felt Andrew slamming himself into me. I knew he loved seeing my ass slap against his body as he fucked me from behind.

I loved getting fucked, and Andrew had gotten accustomed to fucking me like the slut I was, in the bedroom and anywhere else. Including out in public, but the best thing was that he always introduced me by my name. He never said his woman or his girl.

Outside of sex, I was his equal, putting me on cloud nine. He didn't just say it. He acted like it. I had a say in his life, what doctors he was going to, and what projects he would take on. And it was only fair that he had a voice in mine.

"Fuck, yes!" Andrew said as he pushed deep inside of me.

The thing Andrew loved the most other than getting a tit fuck every single day was cumming inside of me. He absolutely loved it.

I felt his grip tighten around my waist as I pushed back hard as he pushed forward. I felt him cumming inside me again for the second time tonight.

I smiled as I looked back at him.

"I was just leaning over the bed to get my phone," I said as I reached out and got my phone.

"Well, it looked so tempting, that I had to," Andrew shrugged.

I had read somewhere that many women didn't like sex from the back. They thought it was selfish of the guy and demoralizing to women.

I didn't know who those women were or why they didn't like it. I loved sex, on my back, on top, behind, whatever the position, I loved it.

My new favorite was behind held while Andrew stood up. I came the most when he impaled me onto his cock and bounced me up and down like a rag doll. And Andrew knew it.

It didn't matter if he was holding me up facing him or when he turned me around with my back toward him. My man could lift my fat ass up and bounce me in either position.

It had been nearly ten months, and we were still going strong, just like Kate and Timothy, but unlike them, we hadn't tied the knot.

Katie looked great in her wedding dress, and Timothy was a handsome groom. Kate rented out her house and was living with Timothy. It was Timothy's idea for her to keep the house, just in case, but as Andrew and I had said, they were a match, always finishing each other's sentences and everything.

Timothy was also a great stepfather to Darold; he was firm, assertive, and a good role model. Darold looked up to him, and I knew he would become a great man because of Timothy's influence.

Then there was Alyssa and Jacob. I thought a kid would bring them closer together, and at first, having a baby girl in their life seemed like a good fit.

Clayton loved his little sister, but things were starting to unravel. Jacob wanted to bring Sistine up one way, and Alyssa wanted another.

The kid was only a few months old, and her parents were already bickering about what college she went to and when it was a good age to give her own cell phone. I knew that if they didn't control things quickly, they would be heading for divorce.

Andrew still did his projects, but his primary source of happiness was working at an animal shelter. He loved working with animals and often got called in to go out and get some stray dog, cat, or other animals.

Andrew said it brought him peace of mind. I liked seeing him with some of the dogs, especially how they loved him. He often got teary-eyed when he either had to say goodbye to them for the last time or had to walk them out to their new families.

I still worked at the bar, and it was also an excellent place to interact with people when I wasn't with Andrew. Everyone knew who I was and who the man in my life was; for the most part, they left me alone.

"Wow," I said as I looked up from pouring a drink out for one of my patrons.

Hank's sister sat down at the bar, she still lived nearby, and I rarely saw her.

"The usual," she nodded.

I nodded back at her as I poured her usual drink out. "Not mine," Linda said. "Hanks," she nodded again.

"Really?" I asked as I emptied the glass and poured out Hank's usual. I gave her the glass, and she chugged it all down. "What's the occasion?" I asked.

"Hank's dead," Linda nodded as she looked at me.

I smiled and shook my head. "Nah, probably on some bender, in some no-name town, like he often does, he will call or message you soon. He always does stupid shit." I laughed.

"No," Linda said as she shook her head. "He's actually dead this time," she said, looking straight at me.

I dropped the glass to the floor. It shattered into pieces.

"What?" I asked. The shock took over me.

"Some guy caught Hank fucking his wife," Linda nodded. "Shot them both with a shotgun, five times," she said as if she didn't believe it herself.

"Holy fuck," I said, leaning against the bar.

"Some town in South Dakota," Linda shrugged. "Never heard of it in my life, but the police called me last night, found my contact information in a rolled-up folder on his bike," she shook her head.

"They lock the guy up?" I asked.

"No, after shooting them, he put the gun in his mouth and blew his head off," Linda said. "Murder, suicide, they are calling it."

"Fuck me," I said.

There wasn't even anyone to go after or anything.

"They only identified him by the leather jacket and his wallet in his pants, that were on the floor," Linda said, shaking her head.

After she said she shot five times with a shotgun, I guessed there wasn't much left.

"I told them they could burn whatever was left, no need to bring it all the way here," Linda said.

"Yeah, no point," I nodded.

Linda stood up. "I thought you should know," she said as she started to walk away.

"Hey, I am here...." I started to say.

Linda shook her head. "I think it would be best if we just didn't pretend, don't you?"

I nodded. We weren't friends. We weren't even close, never had been.

"Thanks for telling me," I said as she nodded and left the bar.

"Holy fuck!" Kate said as I called her, I woke her up, but I needed to tell someone.

"That's what I thought," I said.

"I didn't like him that much, but," Kate paused. "Damn, that's not a good way to go."

I didn't believe it until I looked it up online, and sure enough, there it was. It had made headlines in that part of town. I saw Hank's bike outside the run-down motel.

I knew his escapades were going to get him in trouble. I always thought he would get arrested or badly beat up, but never did I think he would be killed, shot, yes, maybe, but never killed.

"You going to be okay?" Katie asked

"Yeah," I nodded.

Hank was a friend, not good or bad, just a friend. I hated to hear that he got killed, but that's where it ended. I wasn't going to mourn his death long. For now, it was a shock to the system; eventually, it would pass.

"I got to go, that's Jacob on the other line," I said.

"Okay," Katie said.

"Guess you heard," I said as I answered Jacob's call.

"Yup, Linda passed by," Jacob said. "Woke everyone up."

"Yeah, she's going all over," I nodded.

"She kept saying I would be happy to hear," Jacob said.

"She's in shock," I said. "Don't blame her."

"I don't, neither does Alyssa," Jacob said. "What a way to go."

"I know," I said.

"Supposedly they were still you know," I said, "He burst in the room and just shot them while...." I shook my head.

"That's Hank," Jacob said.

"Yeah, it was," I agreed.

Hank would have loved the irony about it all. He would have said something like he was brought into the world between a woman's legs and went out the same way. I smiled as I thought about it. That's the way he lived his life, with no regrets.

"If you need anything, just give us a call," Jacob said.

"I am good, probably going to go down to the bike club tomorrow, and drink a few with his friends, but that's about it," I said.

"Sounds good," Jacob said.

ANDREW LET ME SPEND the night alone, as I wanted to take some time to myself, not because of Hank but because of how fleeting life seemed. One day he was here talking to me; the next, he was blown to bits.

It made me think of all the things I had done in my life or the lack of them; there was nothing to say that Hank Sterling was here. He left no lasting impression on anyone, not a good one anyway.

Sure, he had some unclaimed kids flying around, but nothing made anyone treasure him as a person. I started to think that was going to happen when I passed away.

I looked online and found that the wife and her husband had a six-year-old son. Now that poor kid would go into the system, and who knows how that would turn out for him?

"Wait," I said as I looked back at the picture of the family.

The son looked nothing like his dad. He looked more like Hank. No wonder the father was furious. He had been raising another man's child; maybe he knew or didn't, but that was definitely Hank's kid.

I had a thought, but it wasn't a bad one for once.

IT TOOK SOME DOING and a lot more time than we thought, but it happened. Linda and I were waiting at the airport. It seemed like forever for the doors to open.

First, all the other passengers got off, and most ran to their spouses or friends. Others went by with no one to greet them. Others were calling their bosses or co-workers.

Then we saw him. He was with one of the flight attendants. Linda slowly walked forward. Her eyes said it all. She was both scared and happy.

"Hi," Linda said as she got to her knees.

The kid looked up at the attendant as I gave her all our credentials and ensured she knew we were who she needed us to be.

"I am your aunt," Linda smiled.

It didn't take much convincing on my part to get Linda to adopt the kid. He had no other family anywhere. Linda had no kids of her own, and she loved kids, constantly babysitting other people's kids.

When I told her that Hank had a kid that wasn't claimed and would go into the system, she jumped at the chance.

"What's your name?" the attendant said.

"Adrian," the kid finally said, looking at his aunt.

Linda covered her mouth and then smiled. "That was our father's name," she said as she held out her hand.

Adrian took it, and I nodded. My work here was done, I said to myself as I watched Linda walk with her nephew toward the exit.

"Can we get something to eat?" Adrian asked.

"What would you like?" Linda asked.

"Tacos!" Adrian said.

I smiled and let them go their separate way.

"Finally, a good decision," Jacob said as he was outside waiting for me.

"I think she will be a good parent," I nodded.

Linda and Adrian got in her car and drove off.

"Better than her brother," Jacob nodded.

"Much," I smiled.

We drove back home in silence as we had nothing much to say. I was in a steady relationship that was getting better by the week, and his was falling apart at the seams.

"Okay," I said as I got out of the truck. "Have a good night."

I waved at Jacob as I went inside.

Andrew was waiting for me inside, in the kitchen, making dinner.

"Yummy," I said as I looked over at his food.

"Your favorite," Andrew said.

"Curried Chicken!" I yelled.

I loved it when Andrew cooked. He always made spicy food. It was his specialty. Now that he was learning to cook, he bought many cooking books, predominantly Caribbean recipes.

"I thought you would be hungry," Andrew said.

"Well," I said as I looked at him. "What I am hungry for is not on the stove," I smiled.

"Oh really," Andrew said as he turned down the stove.

I nodded as I got down on my knees.

It didn't take long for me to have his hard cock coursing down my throat. I looked up at him as I sucked on his cock. I loved looking up at Andrew as I pleased him. I loved the look on his face as he watched his woman suck his cock.

I felt his dick as it entered my mouth, over my tongue, and down my throat, it had taken me a while to get used to a thick long cock in my throat, but now it was second nature.

What always followed me taking him this way was Andrew taking control, as he usually did. He grabbed my head and started fucking my mouth, pounding his cock into my mouth and forcing it down my throat.

Andrew's face fucked me relentlessly, using my mouth and throat to get himself off. He fucked my mouth until he finally pushed forward and came hard, grunting and standing on the tips of his toes as he came into my mouth.

"Now, I can eat," I said, looking up at him.

We ate dinner and watched television, he still kept his trailer out there, but most of the time, he slept at my house.

"Do you ever think about it?" I asked as we climbed into bed.

"Think about what?" Andrew responded.

"Having kids of your own?" I asked.

"Not really," Andrew said. "I have Clayton, and Darold, they are like my kids," he shrugged.

It melted my heart how he said that. I knew Clayton loved having Andrew around. The two were always outside, throwing the ball around or playing video games.

I felt bad for taking that option away from Andrew. After Jacob told me about Alyssa being pregnant, I went and got fixed, as people around here would put it. Taking away all chances for any other guy to make me pregnant.

I wasn't in the right frame of mind. I was so mad at Jacob and Alyssa that I decided that if I couldn't have a child with Jacob, then I wouldn't have any with anyone.

"Besides," Andrew said as he smiled at me. "It's a lot of fun practicing making kids," he said as he climbed on top of me.

"Practicing huh?" I smiled as I felt his stiff cock enter me.

"Uh huh," Andrew smiled as he pushed deep into me.

"Keep practicing, all you want," I nodded.

"Now that is an offer I won't turn down," Andrew smiled.

The End

Don't miss out!

Visit the website below and you can sign up to receive emails whenever Alexander Martin publishes a new book. There's no charge and no obligation.

https://books2read.com/r/B-A-NVEDB-EDEYE

BOOKS2READ

Connecting independent readers to independent writers.

Also by Alexander Martin

Adventures With Married Women
Adventures With Married Women: Game Day
Adventures with Married Women: Closing The Store
Adventures With Married Women: Night Flight
Adventures with Married Women: Football Mom
Adventures With Married Women: Gym Heroics
Adventures With Married Women: More Testing
Adventures With Married Women: Further Down the Rabbit Hole
Adventures With Married Women: Other Men's Property
Adventures With Married Women: Never A Dull Moment
Adventures With Married Women: Birthday Treats
Adventures With Married Women: The Wedding Invitation
Adventures With Married Women: Unexpected Invitation
Adventures With Married Women: Dinner Date
Adventures With Married Women: Smarter Decisions

Best Friend's Mom
Best Friend's Mom: Work Life Balance
Best Friend's Mom: Dinner Date
Best Friend's Mom: Moving Out

Black Lake
Black Lake: The Chains That Bind

Crime Does Pay
Follow The Rules
Family Business

Crossroads
Crossroads: Time Waits For No One

From Prude to Whore
From Prude to Whore: Sister Marci
From Prude To Whore: Sister Marci Finale

Gilf Adventures
Gilf Adventures: The Break

Hall Pass
Hall Pass: Another Man's Treasure

Mistakes Were Made

Mistakes Were Made: The Night Out
Mistakes Were Made: Opportunity Gained
Mistakes Were Made: Challenge Accepted

Office Relations
Office Relations: The New Boss
Office Relations: Helpful Boss
Office Relations: The H.R. Meeting
Office Relations: Releasing Tension

Simple Women
Simply Jennifer
Simply Ms. J

The Condo Club
The Condo Club: The Blonde
The Condo Club: The Secretary
The Condo Club: The Maintenance Worker
The Condo Club: The Winning Team

Standalone
A Better View
A Different Kind Of Summer
A Dish Served Cold
A New Direction
Snowed In

Bad Decisions

Watch for more at https://alexander-martin.medium.com/lists.

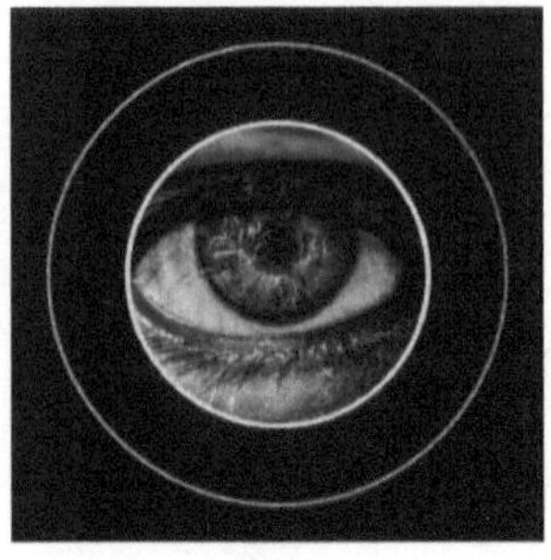

About the Author

I write long and detailed stories that are mostly interracially motivated. I have never been able to write small stories well; I like the how, when, and where. Most of my female characters are independent and strong-minded. I hope most of my readers will leave comments and tell me what they think so I can improve.

Read more at https://alexander-martin.medium.com/lists.